BEARSWOOD END

Suzanne Shephenson

ISBN: 978-1-914965-87-6

Bearswood End

By

Suzanne Stephenson

Also by the author

'Waste' a comic legal novel(coming soon)

Bearswood End   old mine   The high mountains

Logging

The Settlement

Farms   Hunting Camp   The Lake

The river valley

The picnic Place

The Highway   To Town

Bearswood End Region

Introduction...
How I met the Scientist

When we were younger and fitter, and the world seemed full of adventure my husband and myself used to travel extensively. Every time we had time off work to spare, we would go on a trip and find somewhere to explore. Half the fun was discovering quaint hotels, cottages and guest houses and anticipating what we might find. The bit we did not enjoy was the air travel. I specifically hated the queuing at airports and my husband thoroughly disliked the sitting around waiting. However, air travel was a means to an end.

We had gone to Amsterdam for a few days for an anniversary. Since we could only manage a long weekend away from our home commitments at that time, we decided that it would be an ideal place to enjoy for our brief trip. At the end of it we headed for the airport wishing our stay could be longer. Anyone who has ever used Schiphol Airport will know it is a major international interchange for flights from all over the world. So, it came about that we paused near a bookshop and news stand in the airport. There were very few seats in this part of the airport since it was a thoroughfare to different areas of the airport with flights to and from all over the world with a handful of shops in the middle. There was just one bench in front of the bookshop.

My husband expressed a wish to buy a newspaper so he could check investment prices and do the crossword. I sat on the end of the bench which was otherwise unoccupied and had our small items of hand luggage at my feet. He disappeared into the bookshop. I pulled out a booklet from the hand luggage at random. It was one I had obtained at Amsterdam Zoo. I was looking at some pictures of bears when I noticed a man sitting himself down on the end of the bench. He seemed a little flustered.

The man was fairly tall and wore a long brown tweed coat. The collar was pulled up over his neck and lower part of his face. He sported an old-fashioned Homberg type hat which was pulled down. The only bag he carried was a small black holdall. He sat pulling out documents and pieces of paper muttering, "Where are the goddam flight details?" He looked at me and noticed I had heard him.

"Sorry," said the stranger, in English.

I smiled back and said,

"It's difficult sorting out travel documents, I know."

"Yupp… but I think I have them now," he said, and then he saw my booklet. "Do you like bears?"

"Yes, they are probably my favourite animal," I said. "They are attractive animals, and I am sure could be quite scary in the wrong circumstances. I think they are probably brighter than we think, too."

The stranger said, "Then I have something you might like to read," and he took from his bag a small thick notebook with a worn black leather cover and thrust it on my lap. Before I could say anything further, he was gone. I looked about me but could spot him nowhere in the melee of travellers. I opened the notebook. It appeared to be a handwritten diary. There were also several sketches, mostly of bears, dotted about the book.

My husband reappeared carrying a newspaper.

"What is that?" he said pointing at the diary. I told him what had happened.

"Maybe he just went to the gents' toilets," said my husband. "I think we can afford to wait just five more minutes."

But the stranger did not reappear. My husband watched our bags while I went to ask if someone from the bookshop could look after the diary for the stranger until he came back. A young girl at a counter shrugged and pointed at a refuse bin. A man who appeared to be a manager suggested I took it to an airport information desk but pointed in the opposite direction to our direction of travel. By now I knew we needed to get to the gate for our flight.

"No luck?" said my husband.

I shook my head. "I don't think I should throw it away... he may have even intended to give it to me." My husband raised his eyebrows to show disapproval but nonetheless I kept the diary and took it home with us.

I tried putting messages on social media and even contacted 'Lost and found' at Schiphol Airport. No-one claimed the diary so not only did I read it, but in due course I put together a version of the story it revealed. Some pages were water stained or illegible so the story which follows is my attempt to turn the diary into a coherent account. The man, whom I shall call 'the scientist', is the narrator. I hope it is a fair account of his 'adventure' and it follows this introduction.

Chapter 1

Bearswood End Diary

It was spring in the forest. I had decided that this mountainous region was ideal for my research into Brown bears. There was a riot of green and a cacophony of birdsong. It was alive and awake, and I felt alive and awake with every fibre of my being. It was as if I had come out of hibernation just like the bears and other creatures. I was so pleased I had taken a sabbatical from the university to continue my research. This place, a remote settlement, seemed a very promising place, although the locals were a taciturn and wary bunch. Life at the university had seemed stifling. Any research projects appeared tied up in red tape. I did not want to be saddled with a PhD student and a photographer hanging on my coat tails. I wanted to drink in the atmosphere and get a real feeling of how the bears lived their lives. While my scientific papers were accepted by the university and sometimes in well-respected journals, as a person I was dismissed as an oddball and a loner. Today I could not have cared less.

There was no-one at home waiting for me. My dog, a splendid

Dogue de Bordeaux, Duke, had sadly died recently. I had always felt an unreasonable pang of guilt when I left him in kennels. He would look at me with that 'betrayed' countenance as the kennel door slammed shut. Now he was not even waiting for me in kennels. My cats Louis and Henry were used to being left with my neighbour and probably preferred her anyway as she spoiled them with lavish amounts of chicken. Once I had thought there would be another person in the house and eventually a family but settling down with Lizabetta was not to be. But today I am not thinking about her. I am breathing in the heady mountain air with all the scents of spring and concentrating on bears.

There were rumours of a hidden valley and talk of large populations of wildlife hidden away in the mountains above the settlement. It was going to be a difficult place to reach but I intended to find the hidden valley.

That is why this location seemed ideal to me. Although there were roads across the mountain range leading to the settlement, they had a bad reputation. Trucks had been known to jack-knife into ravines never to be seen again. One or two lone travellers had disappeared over the years. Others had been found in mentally confused states and had then left the area hurriedly. The area was off the beaten track and with any luck there would be bears.

I hired a robust vehicle and drove carefully to the settlement where I made my base.

The settlement did not boast many facilities. There was a store with a post office. There was a doctor's office which was visited by a doctor from the regional centre twice a week. There was a vehicle repair garage with a couple of fuel pumps. There were no hotels or motels, but the local bar had three rooms above it which were rented out to visitors. The bar served basic but hearty meals. The settlement was off the tourist trail. The people who lived there eked out a living mainly in forestry. There were a couple of small farms in clearings on the approaches to the settlement but no farms above the settlement. Children were bussed down to a bigger settlement in the valley for schooling or else home schooled.

On the approaches to the settlement there was a small lake with cabins on its shore which were let out to visiting fishermen and hunters, mainly in the summer. There was a small seasonal hunting camp in that area too. Reading online about it, it seemed the hunters were primarily interested in killing deer. A river ran down from the mountains with a series of waterfalls and rapids bursting forth from the blackness of the forest to feed the lake. The lake emptied out into a continuation of the river which rushed down to the valley below. Mountain streams fed into it, so it gradually became wider and less wild in the valley.

The trails from the settlement tended to lead downhill rather than up into the mountains above the settlement, and the area above the settlement appeared to be unmapped. When I expressed the intention of exploring this area in search of the wildlife, particularly for bears, the locals were far from encouraging. There was much sighing and sucking of teeth. It was pointed out to me that I was unlikely to have a mobile phone signal and even if I used any other tracking device the forest was so dense no-one was likely to find me if I became lost or injured. I was warned that not only could I be in danger from the bears I was seeking to study but I might be a tasty meal for a marauding wolf since there were also wolves in these parts.

I explained that I had been in the wilderness before tracking bears and that although I would not be armed, I would take suitable equipment with me to scare off an attack. I was reminded that a bear can accelerate in a sudden burst up to thirty miles per hour. I indicated that after all I might never see a bear. Brown bears need very large territories and adult males are supposed to lead a solitary existence, although my research tended to show that bears tended to live in areas with other bears nearby. The scenes of adult grizzlies congregating together to haul salmon out of the river in Alaska was said to be an exception although matters are never that straightforward. I was going to look for dens where bears had wintered but by now the bears would have left their dens. Even little cubs would have carefully followed their mothers out of their dens.

I was warned not to go; if I did not come back the locals would not look for me. Nonetheless I was determined to go up into the territory above the settlement.

And so, I packed up a knapsack with a compass, a survival blanket, additional water-proof clothing, some water bottles, some high-energy vacuum-packed camping food, some pepper spray, some firecrackers and flares, a minute camping stove, a compressed sleeping bag, a big knife, some matches, a tiny camera, my diary, and a pen. My boots were stout, and my clothing was strong and suitable for mountaineering. My hope was that I would in fact be back before it was dark since I intended to make this initial foray at first light. I did not want to be dinner for a hungry wolf. Nevertheless, I felt I had prepared in case I had to stay out overnight.

Setting off at first light I started to walk on the main path leading upwards from the settlement. Initially, it was wide, and I could see where logging vehicles had left rutted trails. I passed two clearings where loggers had been at work. Eventually the trail narrowed. The trees grew nearer the path and the undergrowth was dense. I could smell the pine trees and pine needles squelched under my feet. There was birdsong and rustling amongst the ground cover. Insects flew into my face. I was pleased I had smothered my neck, arms and legs with repellent. I plodded on and I felt myself getting very warm. I stopped and took off my water-proof jacket and tied it around my waist. As I stood sorting out my clothing, I heard rustling and caught a quick glance of a deer's rump a few feet away. It was a doe with her young. Initially they had no idea I was there but then they bounded away.

Soon the path came to an end at a small cairn of stones presumably placed there to mark the end of the trail and the start of pure wilderness. Beyond the cairn the ground rose steeply. There were outcrops of rocks between the trees. I chose what I thought would be the least precipitous direction and began to climb. After about twenty metres I put a small piece of biodegradable orange ribbon around a narrow tree trunk to help guide me back eventually. Mostly I would use pieces of twig arranged in a cross to mark my path. The biodegradable ribbon would be used very sparingly. I was aware that GPS might not work here.

I appeared to be making good progress clambering up what was becoming an increasingly steep slope. The ground beneath my boots was becoming increasingly challenging. Often stones and scree would slide away beneath me, and I would be in danger of slipping over, but I pressed onwards and upwards. At last, I could see what appeared to be a summit or ridge above. The trees were thinning out and I could even see a small patch of blue sky. Invigorated by the sight of the sky I picked up speed. As I approached the top there a sudden flapping and I had the sense of being slapped in the face by the wing of an immense bird. I lost my footing and caught a glance of the eagle I had evidently disturbed, flying away. I felt myself tumbling to the ground. One of my ankles twanged excruciatingly. I was completely winded and just lay there. I think I blacked out briefly.

As I came round my thoughts were jumbled. I kept thinking of Lizabetta. She and I had met when I was studying for my doctorate. She was just completing her Master's degree. We got on so well together. Everything seemed perfect. We talked of setting up home together, of doing field studies together, particularly of bears as we were both strongly interested in them. Lizabetta was also interested in birds of prey, specifically eagles. There was an irony in the fact that I appeared to have been knocked over by an eagle.

The day came when Lizabetta received a phone call from her home country. Her father was seriously ill, and her mother already had health issues. She said she had no option but to go home. She urged me to go with her, even if it was for a brief visit, but I refused. Some weeks after she left, her father died, and she phoned to say she needed to look after her mother and could not return to the university. She again urged me to visit; she was keen to continue our relationship even though it might be a long distance one. I said I could not come then and that I had too much research.

I never did visit her. I felt jealous of her mother. After about two years I had plucked up the resolve to visit her but as I waited for my plane a tremendous storm blew up and all the planes were grounded. I headed home and did not try to get a later flight. I felt as if the fates had decreed that we were not meant to be together.

Lizabetta continued to send me loving messages for a while. I learned she finished her Master's and was heading up a scientific project at her local university into the preservation of rare eagles. I did not know how to respond to her. Inwardly I knew I had been in the wrong. I just failed to respond and after a while the messages stopped coming. The irony of today was that my fall had been caused by an eagle. That was twelve years ago. I had immersed myself in my work and obtained a prestigious Professorship at my university. I sometimes saw her name in scientific journals so I could have found out what became of her personally. I tried to date other women, but they were generally one-night stands because in my heart I knew there was no-one else like Lizabetta.

Now lying there near the top of the ridge with my ankle in a great deal of pain I realised how wrong I had been. I told myself if I ever got out of the forest I would go and find Lizabetta and even if she had another life, maybe a partner or a husband, even children, just to satisfy myself as to her welfare and apologise to her. I would do that even if I then could be no part of her life. But first I needed to get off the side of the ridge.

I pulled myself free of my pack and wriggled my feet. I sank back and winced. I had done more damage than I had realised. I pulled my pack round so it was partly lying across me so that I could reach inside for something with which to strap up my ankle. All of a sudden, there was a tremendous noise which sounded like the combination of a roar and a yawn. An enormous brown face was looking directly into my face. I could feel the hot damp breath. I had not so much found a bear; a bear had found me. As it will become clear later this was Oskar.

I lay very still. About a 1000 pounds of Brown bear was staring into my face. Surprisingly, he did not touch me. He stood over me and peered into my face so I could not only feel his hot breath but smell the odour of bear. I could see his fierce teeth when he opened his jaws. I could do nothing but lie still and hope that miraculously he would leave alone and not attack me. He made the same roaring, yawning noise again and my heart sank when he was joined by another bear, also apparently a male. I found this most unusual but did wonder if they were going to share me as prey. I dared to peer up and noticed the second bear seemed to have a baseball cap flapping around on the back of his neck. This as I shall explain was Max.

I was beginning to think I was delirious. The bears appeared to look at each other and make noises to each other when the first bear suddenly yanked my collar with his mouth and began dragging me across the forest floor by it. The second bear was dragging my pack along. I found myself yelling, "Woah, oh no, oh no," as I bumped along the ground with the nose of a bear pressed onto the back of my neck and his hot breath on me. I blacked out.

When I came to, I realised that I had been dragged to a much lower level. How my shirt held together I do not know. Only later did I discover I had been dragged over the ridge and was on the lower slopes leading to the hidden valley, next to a rough track. As well as pain from my ankle I felt rather bruised from being dragged across the mountainside. I saw a very battered pick-up truck which looked as if it had once been red but was covered in rust and mud. I found myself together with my pack being bundled into the back of it. I was sure I was delirious because I was sure a bear put me there. If I had seen the driver, I would have been convinced I had lost all touch with reality. The truck went bumping down the track with me in the back. I thought I had been rescued and in a way I had.

Chapter 2

Bearswood End Diary

Oskar the bear seemed to be pulling me out of the back of the pick-up truck. I was pulled gently along by my clothing, and I thought I saw Max climb down from the driver's side of the truck. He appeared to get my pack from the back of the truck. I could see what appeared to be a very old ramshackle collection of buildings. They did not, at first glance, appear to be fit for human habitation. However, I noticed whisps of smoke coming out of the chimney of one of them.

I was pulled inside one of the buildings. It was an old wooden structure. Once I had been manhandled into the rickety building the door slammed shut. It was gloomy but I could see there was light from an old oil lamp. A bearded dishevelled man stood next to a cupboard with what appeared to be medicines in it. Max the bear stood between me and the door. I said to the dishevelled man,

"I think this bear wants to eat me."

"No," said the man. "He wants me to look after you."

"Who are you?" I asked.

"Just call me Doc," was the reply. "Now sit down and let me look at your wounds."

He pointed to a rickety old chair. I did as I was bid. First, he applied some ointment to my face where I had a bruise from the eagle's wing and generally tended to my cuts and bruises. Then he turned his attention to my ankle.

"Can you stand on it?" he asked.

"Hardly at all," I replied and winced when I tried it.

"I can't X-ray it but you seem to have done something quite nasty to it. I shall strap it up. It needs immobilising."

He checked my ankle and foot for cuts. Then several lengths of bandages appeared, and I found my ankle was securely and tightly bandaged. Then a clean but battered tin mug was produced and a couple of white tablets.

"Take these," said Doc. "They are pain killers."

I gulped them down. "Can you hobble over to that couch in the corner?" he gestured. "You can rest there, and I'll bring you something to eat in a bit."

Max made a slight noise.

"It's OK," said Doc to the bear. "You can leave him here. I'll look after him."

The bear made a slight noise and left.

"He'll be back later with some game I expect," said Doc. "I'll get you some soup now."

I settled onto the couch. There were some deerskins. I pulled them over me. Surely, I was having some weird hallucinations? But Doc reappeared with a bowl of soup. It appeared to have venison, root vegetables and berries in it and was rather good.

"Where am I? Whose place is this?" I asked.

"A very long time ago this was a mining village. Now I would say it belongs to the bears." He paused. "However, I suppose you could say this is my house."

"Well who are you? What other people live here? Why don't the bears attack us?" I asked. "How do I know I am not hallucinating?"

Doc replied, "As to your last question only you will know the answer to that. As to your other questions you will understand more given time. You will need to rest and get better. There is an old-fashioned privy in the corner of this cabin. Let me know if you need help getting there. There is plenty of soup. We have venison, mushrooms, dried berries, and some vegetable matter. I even have a tiny stash of tinned peaches and coffee jars, so you won't go hungry or thirsty."

"What is a medical doctor doing in a cabin in the wild?" I queried.

"To be exact I am a veterinary surgeon," came the reply.

I looked puzzled. "What are you doing here? How did you get here?"

"So many questions," said Doc shaking his head.

I noticed how long and shaggy his hair and beard were. His clothing was in part old and worn and in part made of what might have been deerskin.

"I was at a large veterinary practice in the capital for many years. My kids grew up and vets are prone to depression. So, I hit the bottle and my wife left me. I had a breakdown and left the practice, but I took up locum work for an outfit that services the needs of the farms in these mountains. I had been seeing to a cow who had difficulties with birthing a calf. After I left the farm Oskar and Max who brought you here stopped my truck on a lonely piece of road. They brought my truck, my gear and me here. That is my truck you arrived in… At first, I wanted to escape. Then I realised my help was needed, and I had nothing waiting for me at home. Somehow, after a while my depression lifted. My concerns have been more practical, how to get veterinary supplies. It is difficult keeping track of time, but I reckon I have been here about four years now."

I felt more confused than ever, and my face must have conveyed my confusion.

Doc said, "You are in a village populated primarily by bears. You will meet more of them and the few humans who live here in due course. First you have to get better and get used to your surroundings."

I nodded. It was all very strange. I wondered if I would wake up and find myself back in bed in the university. But that of course did not happen.

The cabin was of wood construction but on one side there was a large brick fireplace. The fireplace area was divided in two by some rough brick walling. On one side there was an open fire and on the other side a small metal range fuelled by wood. It looked extremely old. In the middle of the cabin was a wooden table and two rickety wooden chairs. There was no glass in the small window near the main door, which had a heavy wooden shutter which was kept closed for most of the time. In one corner of the cabin there was a door leading to a lean-to structure housing an earth closet or privy. In an opposite corner the area contained a heavy old cupboard where Doc kept his medical supplies. Along the longest wall of the cabin opposite the wall with the main door was my couch and a curtained area where Doc had his sleeping quarters. On one side of the main door was the shuttered window. On the other side of the main door were shelves. On the highest shelves I could see some dried foods such as bags of flour and coffee jars and a number of tins, but nothing looked in the first flush of youth.

There was no electricity, no television, no radio, and no telephone. The lighting was from one small lamp and the fire, except when the main door or window was opened. Doc had a veterinary medical manual, a couple of veterinary magazines and a copy of the Fables de La Fontaine. These had been with him when he had been brought here. The only other reading matter in the cabin was a German-Italian dictionary, two dog-eared National Geographic magazines, a trade directory for motor spares, a body building magazine and a very old bible which may have originated with the builders of the cabin.

I was pleased to find my pack was largely intact since not only did it contain some useful items of clothing but also my notebooks and writing materials. I was therefore able to resume writing my diary.

Doc brought me a makeshift crutch. At first, I was largely confined to the couch and hobbling to the table for meals or to the privy. After about two to three weeks Doc suggested I tested my weight on the ankle and began to encourage me to walk a few short distances a day on it, initially just inside the cabin. After another week he encouraged me to go outside the cabin to a type of covered veranda area. It was here that I became aware of the other human occupants of the village.

It was from the veranda I could see two individuals who appeared to be brothers working or going in and out of a neighbouring building which I assumed they occupied. I asked Doc about them.

"That's Wheels and Stores... the older one is a genius mechanic," he said, "and can fix just about any vehicle or bit of machinery except these darn modern electronics."

"And the younger one?" I asked.

"He is very good at organising and stacking stores," was the reply.

"What are their names?" I persisted.

Doc said, "I don't know, I call them Wheels and Stores and Wheels calls me Doc. Stores is mute. They were here when I arrived. I don't pry. I am guessing that Stores has some issues which might have made it difficult for him to live in the modern world. He is not deaf but for whatever reason he does not speak."

After a few days of going out onto the veranda I received a shy wave and a smile from Stores. He was working on another truck of indeterminate colour outside the barn I took to be part of their home. There was also a very rusty vehicle with its wheels off leaning against an outhouse.

I asked Doc what they were doing.

"Adapting a second vehicle for bears to drive I guess." I did not query matters further at that stage.

From the veranda I could see several dilapidated dwellings in addition to Doc's house and Wheels and Stores' shack. The village was close against the side of the cliff above the valley. It had outcrops of rock above it as well as a number of trees above it. The small clearing beside the cliff had the benefit of a stream gurgling along its edge. I could just about make out a couple of beehives in a flowery meadowed area by the stream which were sometimes attended to by Stores. Then there was thick forest which covered the hidden valley floor. The village was well concealed from prying eyes. So far as I was aware there were no villages and towns between the settlement where I had started this journey and the high mountains, so that all there was on the other side of the secret valley was thick forests, rocks and mountains.

I asked Doc about the origins of the village.

"Gold and silver of course. The mine is well hidden amongst the trees by the cliff-side. It is long forgotten but in its day, I guess this village was full of people trying to get rich."

Only Doc's house and Wheels and Stores' house had wisps of smoke coming out of the chimneys. I saw no other human beings except Doc, Wheels and Stores. The bears Oskar and Max were well in evidence. I saw several other bears including cubs in the vicinity. One day as I was doing some exercises and walking up and down the veranda the two bears Max and Oskar came. Max still had the baseball cap back to front, hanging down the back of his neck. They stood up on their hindquarters looking at me. I stood quite still and waited for an attack which never arrived. Doc came out of the house.

"Hello, boys," he said to the bears. "Have you come to see if he is better?"

Oskar made a slight noise.

"Yes," continued Doc. "He's much better. I can also confirm he really likes bears. He is what humankind call a biologist and naturalist. I think you made a good choice saving him. He is the sort of friend you need."

Max made a slight noise.

Doc continued, "Once he can walk much better, I will show him around and we can then decide what to do next."

The bears seemed to be content and went lumbering away.

"Are they bears you have somehow tamed?" I asked. I then realised it was a silly question for a naturalist, knowing as I do that a bear will always behave as a bear.

"Not exactly," came the reply. "I rather think they have tamed their humans. As you are beginning to learn Max and Oskar are intelligent creatures. You are in their village. They will not harm you because they have understood you will not harm them. They do not harm me because they understand I tend to them if any of them are injured or ill. They do not harm Wheels as I think they sense he is important at fixing things. I think they have a natural affinity with Stores."

It was beginning to dawn on me that all that I thought I had seen was real. This was a hidden place where the bears lived. There were just a few humans who it seemed had chosen to lead secret off-grid lives to help the bears. How much the bears were in control I was yet to discover.

This was indeed the back of beyond, the end of the trail where the bears lived in the woods-- a place which shall be forever Bears' wood end.

Chapter 4

B e a r s w o o d   E n d   D i a r y

As a naturalist I regard myself as guided by the science when it comes to the subject of bears. The two types of bears which held the most fascination for me are Black bears and Brown bears. Black bears are of course widespread throughout North America. Brown bears can be found in both Europe and North America. Grizzly bears are a type of Brown bear who live in certain parts of North America. They are very similar to the European or Eurasian Brown bear. They are just sub-species of the same type of bear known as Ursus Arctos.

Brown bears are the larger animal if one contrasts them with the Black bear. They can be up to 210 centimetres tall and up to 350 kilogrammes. There are some physical differences in their shapes, particularly because Brown bears have very muscular shoulders. Brown bears have very good eyesight although it is thought by some they may only see in black and white. I am not sure I agree with this. They have an incredibly good sense of smell. They need a large territory but unlike the Black bear they find it difficult to climb trees.

Bears do not have opposable thumbs but technically they have five toes on each paw. They have muscles in each toe allowing them to bend their toes. They have fixed claws which are not retractable. Bears can use their paws to shift logs and branches so they can access a food source hidden in a tree or put a log across a stream so they can cross it more easily.

Bears tend to live on their own (except mums and cubs) although very young adult males tend to hang around in pairs. Although bears do not live together, they have been observed co-existing in close proximity to each other. There is a sort of hierarchy with a strong male likely to be at the top and cubs likely to be at the bottom.

Bears communicate with other bears by scent and scent marking. Their vocalisation is limited but I think they will make the same sounds to each other as they will to a human. They are more likely to make grunting and huffing noises caused by expelling air than roaring.

Bears are omnivores. They eat vegetation, berries, fish, insects, and animals. What they eat is to some extent governed by their habitat. During the hibernation period in the middle of winter bears will go for long periods in their dens when they do not eat or drink at all. Naturalist photographers love the scenes of bears congregating together to catch fish during the salmon run.

Bears tend to accumulate fat in the summer and autumn and retire to a den to hibernate for the most severe winter months. Mother bears tend to have their cubs over the winter in the den. They have to rely on their fat reserves to produce milk and to survive. Gestation is six to eight months with mating usually occurring mid-summer. Mothers usually have one or two cubs, but they can have more. Mothers do not stay with their mates after mating and hibernate on their own. They do mate several times with the male before they part company and are inseparable during this period. Later the adult males can become a risk to the cubs.

The cubs will stay with the mother generally until at least two years of age, often until they are in their fourth year. The mothers are tender, loving and protective until it is time for the cubs to leave. Young males tend to spend time together in pairs until they can find their own territory. Young females will often live in an area next to the territory of their mothers'. Brown bears can live for twenty to thirty years but sadly most only live until they are six years old.

As I will explain the village of Bearswood End (as I call it) suited the bears in these mountains very well. And if you are wondering where these mountains might be their location does not appear in this account. I will not say in which continent they are, let alone which country. I do not say in which country the settlement of humans is situated nor do I say in what language I conversed with Doc or anyone else. Without wanting to sound big-headed I do speak several languages. Whether the location is Europe or North America, or Asia I am not saying. I do not want this secret place discovered. These bears should not become curiosities to be gawped at and prodded.

Their village has about thirty buildings and the entrance to the old mine. Some buildings were disused. Closest to the homes of Doc and Stores and Wheels was a single-storey house. At first glance it looked in poor shape. The front door was open and half off its hinges, but several large bushes had grown up near the open doorway affording it some shelter from the wind. The rest of it looked sound. On closer inspection one could see several items of furniture had been piled up just inside the doorway, whether accidentally or on purpose. There was an aperture in the pile of furniture for a bear to get in and out.

This was the home of Gerda and her cubs Saul and Selma. I did not know if she had denned here for the winter or had come to the house more recently.

The cubs were only a few months old. It was good to see them playing in the spring sunshine. Gerda's home was some distance from any adult males.

Her nearest neighbour lived in what must have once been a two-storey house. Now the upstairs had caved in together with the roof but a sound looking single storey annex which might have been a kitchen as it had a stone chimney was still standing and was the home of Alice, Toffee and Fudge. Toffee and Fudge were young males, about a year old, still dependent on their mum, but learning the ways of the bear-world.

Just next door to Alice in what might have once been a barn lived two young females Juno and Julia. There was a ramshackle hut nearby which housed Olivia and a tiny frail looking cub Una.

The males lived the other side of the stream in a cluster of buildings near the entrance to the old mine. Oskar and Max lived in a shack there. Two young males Frank and Ivor had another shack. There were at least two more structures on the edge of the village that side of the river and two bears lived there. It was good that there was space between these buildings and the other bears since they housed an older male each, Ivan (the Terrible) and Peter (the Great).

I might add that the names were those used by Doc and myself to identify the bears when we were talking about them. I do not believe in anthropomorphising animals, but it just seemed right to use these names and indeed as I found out if I called out to Max there did seem to be a gleam of recognition that I meant him.

We called Ivan, 'the Terrible' because he was the fiercest and most unpredictable bear. By contrast Peter 'the Great' had a better demeanour but he was the largest bear in the whole village. Ivan looked battle-scarred and had a fearsome reputation for winning out with the females. On the other hand, he tended not to pick fights with Peter the Great due to Peter's immense size. Ivan and Peter were probably the fathers of most of the cubs in the village. Doc expressed concerns over Olivia and Una. If Olivia came into heat in the summer, he felt it was possible Ivan might kill Una in his anxiety to mate with Olivia. He thought Oskar might have fathered Una.

Max and Oskar interacted most with the humans, followed by Juno and Julia. Max and Oskar as I will further explain were very interested in the trucks. Juno and Julia would shyly come to see if we had any tasty extra bits of food but were not averse to reciprocating. Once or twice, they had left a slightly squashed fish on the veranda.

One sunny morning Gerda appeared in a distressed state. Selma was at her side, but Saul was hanging back holding his paw in the air. Blood was oozing from it. Gerda was huffing and swaying from side to side. Doc made encouraging noises and made a big effort to coax the little cub forward. Eventually we had the cub on the veranda. It soon became clear he had a bit of old barbed wire stuck in his claw.

"Oh dear, I thought we'd got rid of most of that stuff," said Doc as he sprayed some analgesic spray on the paw and speedily pulled the wire away. Saul would have made off then, but Gerda nudged him back.

"She knows I will say when I have finished," said Doc. He quickly cleaned the paw and applied an antibiotic injection.

"Finished now," he said. Gerda took her cubs back to her den.

"He was so good," I said. "Where do you get the antibiotics?"

"He does what his mother expects. As for the antibiotics... just with other medical supplies. It is difficult. Essentially, we steal them…"

I nodded.

"As you know Max and Oskar can drive adapted trucks after a fashion. They seem to really like doing so and will often hang about near Wheels and Stores waiting for an opportunity. Now and then we send them usually with Stores down to that town in the valley. They break into one of the pharmacies. It's a bit of a mixed bag what might come back but it keeps us going. A bigger problem is fuel. Wheels and Stores always have a can with them and never miss an opportunity to siphon off some fuel. We do have a tanker which Max and Stores hijacked quite a long time ago, up on the trail, but its contents won't last forever, and I don't think something like that can be repeated."

I did not feel as surprised as I might have done a while ago.

"Do they steal anything else?" I asked.

"I understand that the bears used to run large trucks and wagons off the road using fallen trees and drivers would sometimes get badly injured or worse. Wheels and Stores managed to dissuade them. Although they tend to like beer and fizzy pop, the authorities were beginning to investigate. These days the bears understand it is not good to attract too much attention. We discourage them from bad behaviour and try to attract as little attention as possible. The bears are very keen on baked goods. Twice they forced the baker's van to stop when it was on the way to the settlement. The van driver was no doubt terrified when two huge bears blocked the road and then broke into the back of the van. Fortunately, they did it near the river valley so initially the authorities searched for bears in that area. However, they have not done it again. These days the bears make occasional forays to the supermarkets and bakeries on the outskirts of the town in the valley in the dead of night. The supermarkets often ditch slightly out of date food into outside bins which helps. Now and again though Oskar and Max will break in and steal bread and rolls mainly."

"Is it just Oskar and Max who go on these expeditions?" I asked.

"Juno and Julia are learning the ropes of the expeditions to the town these days, so they sometimes go with Oskar, Max and Stores. Peter the Great is involved in stopping vehicles if needed. He just has to stand in the road. Gerda used to help out with things before she had cubs. All the bears keep away from the settlement," explained Doc. "These days we organise visits to towns in the valley. Ivan the Terrible behaves most of the time although last year he took a cow from one of the farms below the settlement. There was a bit of a hue and cry but fortunately the farmers thought the bear which attacked the cow came from along the river valley as there had been some reports of bears in that area."

"The bears seem to understand that Wheels, Stores and yourself are here to help them but does that ever go wrong?" I queried.

Doc answered, "Well, it hasn't done yet although we are all particularly careful of Ivan the Terrible. It is usually best to make sure he has a full belly first if anything tasty is brought back to the village."

Doc continued with his tasks, and I made further notes about these amazing bears. The weather continued to warm, and carpets of vegetation appeared on the forest floors. Mushrooms and edible herbs and foliage were available for harvesting and eating. I continued to heal and increase my mobility. As I sat on the veranda, I happened to say how idyllic it all appeared.

Doc responded,

"Yes, but we live on a knife edge of avoiding people. I can but hope the spring does not bring out more hunters. Mostly they hunt deer down in the valley but occasionally when the conditions seem better, we get some amateur who fancies looking for bear at higher levels."

"What do you do?" I asked.

"Mostly we try to hide ourselves and the village. There are a number of strategies which have worked so far," he responded.

I did not ask about those strategies, but I was to discover them later.

I could appreciate the need to keep this wonderful place secret. The bears' home was a special place. I noted that in the area wildlife was in abundance. I could see eagles wheeling above and other birds of prey. Now and again, I glimpsed wolves between the trees, but they never actually entered the village. The sparkling stream was now full of small fish and there was a hum of bees amongst the wildflowers which were presenting a colourful carpet. They also buzzed busily around the hives.

I extended my sphere of activities as I became stronger, strolling around the village and making notes and sketching the bears. I did not go into their houses as I thought entering an inhabited bear's den was asking for trouble. The females, the cubs and Oskar and Max did not seem to mind in the slightest. They would often walk or sit within feet of me without a hint of aggression. Sometimes I might chuck them a tasty morsel, some honeycomb gathered from the hives, or mushrooms I had found. They did not seem to care if I sat on a rock making notes or a quick sketch.

On one occasion I did have a fright. I accidentally got a little too close to Ivan the Terrible's home. I think I was lulled into a false sense of security by the good nature of the other bears. As I was ambling in the sunshine in the woods, I passed Ivan and Peter's houses. Ivan the Terrible suddenly appeared in front of me from behind some trees. He was standing up on his hind legs just a few feet from me. His growl sounded more like a roar to me. There was saliva dripping out of his mouth. I could see his teeth and they looked capable of tearing me limb from limb in an instant. I froze. For a few seconds I thought I would meet my end at the hands of this bear who seemed truly savage and primeval. Then, there was a low, loud growl from behind me. Peter the Great was standing up behind me. He looked absolutely massive. His growling seemed to be directed not at me but at Ivan the Terrible. In fact, whether I imagined it, I don't know, but I could have sworn he was pointing with his paw for me to make my escape. Indeed, I exited in the direction I thought he was pointing and made my way back to Doc's house.

Doc noticed I looked shaken, so I told him what had happened. I asked him if Ivan the Terrible and Peter the Great would have had a fight.

"No, once you had gone, there would be nothing to fight about. But you must be more careful. Ivan the Terrible is not to be trusted. Indeed, you must not forget these are all wild animals. Some people just regard them as game to be hunted."

His words were quite prophetic.

Chapter 4
Bearswood End Diary

Ivan the Terrible was beginning to court Juno. He would not let anyone near her. She shyly reciprocated. Soon they were inseparable. Juno moved across the river to Ivan's shack.

Stores had been on a brief expedition one night with Max and Oskar to the valley. They came back with a few medical supplies, two cans of fuel and a large box of out-of-date burger buns, presumably from a raid of the bins. Stores seemed very agitated. He was gesticulating to his brother who had not gone with him. After a while Wheels told Doc and me that Stores had noticed considerable activity at the hunting camp with vehicles and men heading that way.

"What do you think?" I asked.

Wheels and Doc both agreed great care was needed. We would have no fires for the next few days. The vehicles would be concealed by tree branches and foliage. The houses and shacks in good condition would have branches and foliage placed over them. The beehives would be covered in foliage. If anyone made it to the ridge it would therefore be difficult to see the village from above. The geography helped conceal it, but chances could not be taken.

Max, Oskar and Julia supervised by Stores were also sent to cover up the tyre tracks which might have led to the village. The bears seemed instinctively to know that the cubs should not be let out to play. They kept to their houses. Going out for food or to interact was left until after dark.

"How long will we be like this?" I asked Doc. The reply was not reassuring.

"Until they get bored and go away."

We had been in this stealthy mode for about five days when one night I woke up in the middle of the night with an awful feeling of foreboding. I was covered in a cold sweat and the back of my neck prickled. I could not get back to sleep.

In the early hours of the morning a shot rang out from the ridge above us.

"Shit," said Doc. "The hunters are above us. Sounds like someone was trigger happy though. But I think everyone is in the village. They have done us a favour. At least we are warned."

He went out to the veranda and made a low cooing noise and said quietly, "Hey, bears, hey bears… Oskar, Max, Peter… hey bears."

After about five minutes Oskar and Max and Peter the Great appeared. They almost hugged the ground so that in the early morning near darkness they were barely visible.

"Tell the girls and cubs to stay inside," he said to the bears. "We also need some false trails laying, away from the settlement. Are you able to persuade Ivan to help?"

There was a muffled grunt from Peter. I believed that he understood what was being said.

"Do you think he could get out the other side of the valley and make his way down to the farms without being seen? Could he take a cow then and leave a trail along the river valley?"

There was another muffled acknowledgement.

"He will have to be careful not to get followed back here so he may need to stay in the river valley for a bit. And the three of you need to leave scat and scratch tree bark in directions away from this place... but be very, very careful."

The bears crept away into the darkness.

"Did they understand you?" I asked. "Will Ivan help?"

"I believe they will do their parts," replied Doc. Although there is no way of proving they understood I was sure they had taken in the plan.

I learned later that Ivan the Terrible had more than done his part. He had managed to make his way past the hunters without attracting attention and had focused on the farms below the settlement. One farmer had placed his herd out to summer pasture. Ivan had taken down an unfortunate heifer and not to put a fine point on it had then feasted upon her. I am not sure if his actions in respect of the other farm came before or after he dined on heifer, but in the event, he broke into a milking parlour which was, fortunately for the cows, unoccupied. He managed to break open a small tank of milk and cause a terrible mess. He probably enjoyed what he could of the milk but from the point of view of the hunters, attention was drawn away from the mountains above the settlement.

The farmers were incensed with anger. Why were the huntsmen on a wild goose chase further up the mountains? There was plainly a 'bear problem' lower down.

Meanwhile Max, Oskar and Peter had been busy laying false trails.

Max and Oskar came back to the settlement as soon as they could, but Peter remained at large. Bears and humans with the exception of Peter the Great and Ivan the Terrible hid in the village.

Initially the pop of gunfire could be heard in the distance. The hunters moved away presumably following the false trails, but as I learned later, they were also following reports of the attacks on the farms and reports of "an enormous bear" near the road from the settlement down to the valley.

Peter was clearly being his imposing self to try and scare the hunters but also to bravely lead them away. I worried when he was away from the village for such a long time and the hunters were at large, and I got the impression that Doc, Wheels, and Stores shared my concerns. There also seemed to be some disquiet amongst the bears. I had not seen Juno for several days, but I had assumed she had kept within either the shack she shared with Julia or the shack she had been sharing with Ivan. After Ivan returned, instead of spending time in his den presumably with Juno he had started pacing backwards and forwards near the perimeter of the village, appearing very distracted and making huffing, groaning and growling noises. Before long Doc and I realised Juno was missing. We concluded she must have followed Ivan the Terrible when he went to the farms. Now we were fearful that harm had befallen her.

All we could do was wait and worry.

Eventually Peter the Great returned. He seemed unfazed by his experience. The area close to the village seemed quiet. Wheels and Stores took a truck out and did a reconnoitre and seemed satisfied the hunters had left the area. Bears began to emerge, and we took away the camouflage, but still Juno was missing.

Days passed. Ivan the Terrible continued pacing. I was worried he might turn his attentions to another female, particularly Gerda. However, I truly felt he had a despondent look. Wheels and Stores searched close to the village in case Juno was nearby, but she was nowhere to be seen. They did not search further afield for fear of being spotted but also through not knowing where to look.

One day when I had given up on the prospect of Juno returning there was a crashing and scrunching noise in the undergrowth near Doc's house. An exhausted, dishevelled and wounded Juno literally dragged herself out from between the trees and lay panting and groaning on the ground in front of the veranda. There was dried blood on her shoulder. Her fur was matted. Her nose looked dry and grey.

"I think she has been shot," said Doc. "It's a miracle she made it back here. She looks in a sorry state."

Stores said that he would check to see if she had been followed. We had the immediate problem of how to treat her wounds. Not only was there a question of how you treat a wounded bear anyway, but also, we were concerned about the potential interference from Ivan.

Ivan the Terrible started pacing up and down close to where she lay but Peter the Great and Max and Oscar placed themselves between Juno and Ivan.

Doc produced two syringes and two small bottles from a locked box which was more or less sunk into the floor near an outside wall.

"I hope this stuff has kept as I don't have a fridge," he said. "I have a little local anaesthetic and the other is antibiotics. It is the only anaesthetic I have left." He looked concerned.

We both approached Juno and he gave her the shot of anaesthetic as I was saying in what I hoped were soothing tones, "Hey, bear, hey, Juno... we are here to help."

"Ideally I could do with a dart gun with anaesthetic," Doc said. He started to probe her wound. She was only semi-conscious, and the anaesthetic obviously helped numb her shoulder.

I repeated the refrain, "Hey, bear, hey, Juno we are here to help."

"As I thought," Doc said. "She has been shot. Let's hope the bullet is not too far in."

He worked extremely quickly cutting back some fur on her shoulder and cleansing the area.

"Good thing it's in her fatty area," Doc mused and producing a clean sharp knife from his pocket, made a quick incision and removed the bullet. Then he gave Juno an antibiotic injection and slapped a poultice of leaves on the wound to stem any bleeding.

"These particular leaves have disinfecting qualities," he said. "Although I do hope she keeps still."

She lay there in the afternoon sun for about two hours recovering while Peter, Max and Oskar stood guard. Eventually she stumbled to her feet and made off towards Ivan. Doc said in whispers from the veranda, "I'm glad she has got up, I was beginning to think she was too far gone."

"Will she be okay with Ivan?" I said.

"Who knows, who knows?" replied Doc as Ivan and Juno headed into Ivan's shack together.

Next day she failed to emerge but there was the sound of more than one bear grunting and growling from inside the shack. We did not dare get too close. Ivan did eventually come out. He disappeared for a couple of hours dragging back the body of a doe. He stopped outside the shack and ate some tender morsels of deer. The rest he pulled into his dwelling.

"Well, that is a surprise," said Doc. "I never thought Ivan would hunt for anyone other than himself."

Ivan and Juno spent the next few days together in his shack.

Eventually, one still summer's day both animals emerged. Ivan looked fierce as ever. Juno was strolling about normally but looked thin and out of condition. Doc, Wheels, Stores and I did our best to throw some tasty titbits into Juno's path: fish, fruit, mushrooms and herbs. Surprisingly, Ivan made no attempt to take the little extras. I believed that most likely it was a matter of instinct due to having chosen her to have his cubs. It was a while before she looked fully recovered but she was clearly resilient and recover she did.

Doc expressed concerns about the reduction in his medical supplies. I asked the question,

"Are we done with hunters for now?"

Doc's response was slightly despondent. "I hope so but at some point, others will come. To me it is so senseless when you consider how magnificent these bears are."

I nodded to show I understood.

Some sort of peace had descended on the village. Oskar was hanging around Olivia a great deal, yet he was surprisingly gentle around Una. Peter the Great was Julia's constant companion.

More than ever, I appreciated why Bearswood End should be kept secret. These animals were intelligent and resourceful and deserved to be left alone. I understood if farmers became angry if they lost livestock but there seemed nothing comprehensible in hunting these wonderful creatures for sport. Further, as they seemed so intelligent, I had come to the conclusion I did not want hordes of scientists descending on beasts who were in effect my friends to poke and prod and analyse them. I would certainly record my adventures, but I was concerned about what might be said in the public domain. There was other wildlife in the vicinity which deserved to be left alone including the eagles and the wolves I had seen. I was aware that attention from naturalists could be a mixed blessing for animals. In Africa poachers often congregated just outside the Wildlife Parks. In Churchill, Manitoba, the Polar bears had become a tourist attraction and subject to photographic visits from especially designed buses, whether they minded or not. As a naturalist myself I was not necessarily in agreement with some of my brethren. While studies to demonstrate climate change might have seemed laudable on the surface, I hated the thought of holding a camera on some creature just to show it was dying of lack of water because the local water hole had dried up. Rather, I felt empathy with my bear companions for example, and I was thinking of ways of aiding them.

At some point I felt I might return to the wider world, but I was in no hurry to do so. I needed to decide the purpose of doing so and indeed what was best for the bears rather than just what was best for me, although I had a feeling that what might be best for them might also be what was best for me. Any decision to return even for a short time ought to be made before winter.

Chapter 5

Bearswood End Diary

It took a while for things to settle down in the village. I took time to think and to go through my personal property which had been in my knapsack, and clothing. I found that there was some cash which although not a great deal could prove useful. There was one of my credit cards and some identity documents. There was a mobile phone but that was broken. I still wore my wristwatch which although having a badly scuffed face, still ran. I must have left the rest of my documents and further bank cards in the room I had taken in the settlement. I was pleasantly surprised by the items I had discovered and formulated a plan to help the bears. I might then consider returning to the world for a bit.

I explained to Doc what I intended to do.

"They don't know me in the town in the valley," I said. "So, if I tidy myself up, I can do a little shopping. Wheels or Stores can drive to somewhere just out of town and wait for me. At the very least I can use the cash. However, if no-one has reported me dead or missing to the credit card company, I can use my card. I will go shopping in different places. If the pharmacy is not too fussy, I might be able to get some antibiotics. I will feign a sinus infection…"

I explained in quite some detail what I had in mind. At first Doc shook his head and was dubious but eventually I won him over. We then put my plan to Wheels and Stores who initially had doubts.

Wheels said, "I know a place where I can hide the truck, but I don't want to be there too long. There will have to be a time-limit. If you are not back within three hours, I am afraid you will be stuck there."

I nodded in acknowledgement.

Doc helped me clean myself and my clothing up. I made a mental note to add soap and a few t-shirts for Doc, Wheels, Stores and myself. It was an ever-growing list. My hair was cut to some degree with an old rusty pair of scissors, and I trimmed my beard too. There was no mirror, so I had to rely on Doc for guidance.

When we drove off to town, we set off very early in the morning so few people in the settlement were around. In the early morning light those who were awake would have assumed Wheels was a logger passing through. We drove down the mountain road from the settlement and as we got a little lower, we passed entrances to farms and paddocks of grazing cattle. We passed the entrance to the hunting camp and crossed over the bridge of the gushing river which gurgled, sprayed and slurped over the rocks. Further down the slopes there were woods of deciduous trees and as we entered the valley there were orchards and some vines being cultivated on lower slopes. On the valley floor there were green pastures and the river snaked through it, widening out. There was another bridge over the river with thickets of trees each side of the water.

There was a picnic area just before we crossed over the bridge. It must have been a pleasant spot for families to picnic in the summer, with wooden benches and tables and views of the river. Morning mist billowed over the river. Wheels crossed over the bridge passing the picnic area and suddenly pulled off the road into the thicket of trees, and we bumped along between the trees and bushes before he stopped. I could see this was far more secluded than the picnic area.

"I'll wait here," he said. "Not too far for you to walk into town. If you are not back in three hours I'm going."

I nodded. I slung my empty knapsack over my shoulder and made for the road. As I trudged along the side of it more traffic seemed to appear. Eventually the road from the mountains intersected with a large highway which was full of traffic which gave no quarter. I paused for a minute and considered how to proceed. When I had come this way many weeks ago, I was of course driving the hire vehicle which I had collected from the regional airport, which was altogether different.

I could see that if I managed to cross this highway there was a smaller road leading off it, in the distance which led to the built-up outskirts of the town. I awaited a slight pause in the traffic and ran across the highway to much honking of horns by trucks. Having survived crossing the highway I was relieved to see there was a substantial supermarket, some might call it a hypermarket, not far down the smaller road. I had been going twenty minutes on foot. I walked speedily past the large carpark.

There was an ATM close to the supermarket entrance. I tried my card in it. To my pleasant surprise it worked. If anyone reported me missing it had not got through to the bank.

The supermarket had just opened its doors presumably for workers on early shifts. I took a trolley. First, I headed for the luggage section.

I selected a small black suitcase with wheels, the type of holdall you see used by airline cabin crew. Then on to the clothing section. I put into the trolley eight pairs of under pants of differing sizes, sixteen pairs of socks, and eight T-shirts of differing sizes so the humans in the village would be better clothed.

I entered the toiletry and pharmacy aisles. The trolley was becoming piled up. I added a pack of toothbrushes, half a dozen toothpaste tubes, a box of soaps, a dozen crepe bandages and several wound dressings, surgical tape, some sharp scissors, some small pliers, some tweezers, some tubes of antiseptic cream, a jar of Vaseline, some basic painkillers, some antihistamine tablets, some cans of insect repellent, some surgical wipes and a bottle of disinfectant. I decided to head for the checkout and as a row of checkouts came into view, I passed a magazine rack and a cabinet displaying snacks for people who might want to grab a quick lunch. I also grabbed a large canvas shopping bag which had the supermarket's logo stuck in the middle of it in a garish orange next to a picture of a somewhat incongruous smiling orange monkey.

I quickly chose a magazine about trucks and cars and added two energy drinks to the trolley. I also tossed in the largest sandwich I could spot and a handful of chocolate energy bars. The young girl at the check-out looked at me suspiciously.

"I'm going abroad to the jungle," I blurted out which probably sounded even more suspicious, but my credit card worked, so all was well.

I stopped in the foyer to the supermarket where there were some seats, close to a bakery stall and a noticeboard. There were enticing smells from the bakery, but I resisted temptation. I packed my shopping into the knapsack and small suitcase. There was a noticeboard just above where I was sitting. I took a mental note of the address of a walk-in medical clinic. This seemed to be somewhere near the centre of town.

As I left the supermarket, I noted there was a taxi rank outside.

I decided it was time to head back to Wheels and the truck.

After crossing the busy road, the rest of my trudge seemed relatively uneventful, albeit I was slowed down a little by wheeling the little case. Wheels was still very much there.

"You've only been two hours," he said.

"How can you be so sure?" I asked. He pointed to the truck against which he was leaning.

"Dashboard clock works after a fashion," he said. "Plus where the sun is," he added.

"Well, I need another two hours," I said.

"What am I supposed to do?" said Wheels scowling.

I tossed the magazine and the sandwich to him and then passed an energy drink and energy bar to him.

I put the small suitcase in the truck, and I then took the shopping from the knapsack and put it in the monkey shopping bag and put that in the truck as well. My knapsack would be needed for the next part of my expedition. I sat for a few minutes quaffing from my can of energy drink and munching on an energy bar. I still felt very tired, but I wanted to complete what I saw as a mission.

I trudged back to the supermarket and got into a cab. I gave the driver the address of the walk-in clinic. It took just five minutes to reach the address which was in a pleasant square which fortuitously also had a taxi rank. I paid the driver some of my precious cash and began looking for the clinic. I soon spotted it in a modern white building, next to a row of little shops in an older building. The shops included a sporting and camping goods' store, and a small store selling phones and other electronics. There was a little wooden decorated cabin just outside the modern building selling postcards and tourist souvenirs.

I entered the clinic and spoke to a uniformed receptionist. I weaved a tale of being a visitor to the area and suffering from sinusitis and asthma. To my pleasant surprise I was given an appointment in just thirty minutes time. I said I would return.

I paid cash in the phone shop for a couple of used mobile phones. I bought sim cards and paid for some cards to get minutes on them, and I also bought a charger which could be plugged into Wheels' truck dashboard all for cash. Then I stepped in the camping goods' store and bought insect repellent, a starting pistol which I was told would make a good bang, and four pairs of heavy-duty trainers. In my case I had the luxury of trying on my shoes, but with the others I had to guess. Everything just fitted in my bag.

I went back towards the clinic making sure I walked swiftly not just for time but to build up a sweat. I was shown into a young female doctor. As I thought she might, she took my temperature and my pulse.

"Your pulse is just a little fast," she said. "And your temperature is only slightly raised but I can see you look flushed. Fortunately, your oxygen level looks near enough normal."

I gave her quite a convincing performance of having a sinus infection and expressed my concerns over my asthma (the reality being I have not had asthma since I was a child).

She said,

"I will give you fourteen days of a broad-spectrum moderate dose antibiotic. If your asthma gets worse, you may need a steroid tablet."

I made a great thing about the extent of my travels and how difficult it was to get medical attention. I managed to walk out with a twenty-eight-day course of antibiotics and ten days' worth of steroid tablets. I was sure Doc would find them very useful.

Before I left the area, I stopped at the souvenir cabin to see what their postcards were like. There was a lot of tourist tat but also one or two small carved ornaments. They were of a mixture of figures of eagles and bears. I was taken aback by one slightly larger carving. It was about six inches long. It was a representation of a car with a bear sitting in the driver's seat. I decided to buy it so as to make an excuse to ask about it.

The stall holder said,

"Local gossip has it bears have been seen driving vehicles up in the mountains. It's just drunks imagining things but the tourists like the idea, so we get a few carvings like this in stock from time to time."

I tried to look impassive and said, "Well I will buy it as a bit of fun."

I THEN GOT A CAB to the supermarket. I noticed someone had left a football on the backseat. I mentioned it.

"Take it," said the driver. "I don't want some kid's old soccer ball. Think yourself lucky it's not an old pair of pants."

I took the ball. Somehow, I thought of Max and Oskar.

I had one last errand before I made haste to find Wheels. I went to the bakery in the foyer to the supermarket. I bought a bag of twenty bread rolls and a bag of twenty apple pastries.

"Big picnic," I said smiling as I paid. I just about got the rolls in my knapsack, but not the pastries. I put the pack on my back and had a perilous time crossing the road with a heavy bag on my back, some pastries in my right hand and my left hand cradling the football. Then I trudged back to Wheels.

He smiled immediately he saw the football.

"Yup," he said, "I think some bears will love playing with It... and they'll gobble up the pastries in seconds."

I told him about the starting pistol, and how I hoped it might frighten away unwanted predators and bears not belonging to our village. I showed him the phones and the shoes and told him how I fared at the clinic. I indicated I was aware of the reception problems in the remote areas, but I still felt they would be useful. I mentioned the carving. Then I asked him to make haste back to the village. I was absolutely exhausted and slept most of the way back.

My shopping was a great success except I clearly did not have enough pastries and buns. Purist naturalists who had not come across bears with the traits of my friends would have no doubt been appalled by the bears having sweet pastries anyway.

Max and Oskar purloined the ball but some of the cubs came to look as well and made exploratory pushes of it.

I made three more trips to town over the next few weeks as summer imperceptibly slipped by. I warned Doc, Wheels and Stores that plainly a bear or bears had been seen driving and care had to be taken. The carving sat on a shelf in Doc's house. Sometimes I would show it to Max and Oscar and say,

"People have seen you. Please be careful."

They would look into my eyes as if they understood. I really hoped they did.

On one visit to town, I spotted some warm jackets in a summer sale and bought three for Doc, Wheels and Stores. I bought some footballs. I purchased more basic medical supplies. I bought a range of tinned and dried foods and bags of rolls and pastries (which I knew would not last). I bought a couple of cans of fuel which I told the filling station was for taking to farm machinery.

I did not dare go back to the same clinic, but I found a small, doctor's surgery and spun the same yarn and came away with another fourteen days of antibiotics. I discovered a pet supplies' store. Some pet medication could be bought over the counter so I bought what I could. I found a hardware store and bought a small toolkit including hammer and nails to supplement tools in the village. My most expensive purchase was a portable camping fridge, some solar panels, and a generator to go with the panels. To get them to Wheels' truck I took a taxi to the picnic area just the other side of the bridge. That day I also bought a 20 litre jerrycan and filled it with fuel.

"My friends will come soon with their campervan," I said as I paid the taxi driver who fortunately did not seem interested.

Wheels waited for it to become dusk before meeting me and loading up. I knew the fridge would be helpful to Doc when things became warm on a sunny day. The generator would also help with phone charging.

On my last shopping trip to town, I bought some more credit for the phones in the village, and I bought myself a phone. I went into an internet café and checked my finances. I was fortunately able to access my bank account since I have a good memory for passwords. To my pleasant surprise the university had continued to pay my basic retainer salary, although obviously not the add-on I used to earn for lecturing and tutoring. Regular payments had continued to service the credit card. My finances could have been in a worse state but plainly I needed to take some action. With some trepidation I tried to access my main email account.

There were hundreds of emails. There was no way I could go through them.

I looked at my university email account. There were fewer emails. I noticed there was a recent one from the Dean of Faculty. Its contents were not unexpected. It said I had far exceeded my leave of absence for scientific research. It added if I did not return by the start of the next academic term my services would be terminated for 'gross misconduct' with immediate effect.

It was time to make plans.

Chapter 6
Bearswood End Diary

I knew we were into autumn. Over the winter the bears would hibernate in their houses. I understood the humans' activities would be much curtailed since when the worst of the snow and ice were at hand they would do their best to keep warm in their houses. Doc and Wheels and Stores were building up stocks of logs. If there was a mild spell occasionally some bears might come out for some supplemental food, but it was explained to me that the village by and large closed down for the winter.

In the really bad weather, the settlement and the logging camps became inaccessible, let alone the village of Bearswood End. It made the tanker of fuel (hijacked sometime in the past) hidden away on the secret trackway from the village, inaccessible so the trucks could not be refuelled.

Doc explained, "We are fortunate, however, that being at the bottom of this valley we are in a sheltered protected spot. There is a kind of microclimate which makes it milder here than up on the ridge or indeed where the settlement is. Nonetheless, it is quite a harsh place to be in the winter, albeit beautiful."

I sat on a rock one afternoon close by the stream and adjoining meadow. Max and Oskar sat with me. A football lay in the grass.

"Listen," I said, "I will have to go away for a while. I need to visit the big world and sort some things out."

The bears appeared to put their heads on one side. Max moved closer to me until he was sitting right next to me. In the past I might have been terrified but now I was happy to carry on talking.

"I need to sort out my life, but I intend to come back here. I need to visit a lady. Humans often have mates so it would be like one of you visiting a female, although I don't know if she will want to have anything to do with me. If I can sort out my life, I want to bring back some useful things too… I promise I won't bring hunters and I really want to come back."

Max looked sad and remarkably laid his enormous head against my legs.

I said, "Hey, Max, you are a good bear, and in your own way I think you understand what I am saying." I had no way of knowing if this was true, but we sat together for quite a while.

I started to make preparations to leave over the next few days. I talked with Doc and Wheels how we could use the mobile phones to keep in contact. Until the village was snowed in, and Wheels could not get to a place with a signal we would send brief texts weekly, which would resume after the thaw. When I returned, I would try to make contact by text first. I did not want anyone to follow me onto the secret trails leading to the village.

I asked Doc to further clip my hair and beard for me. He raised his eyebrows and did a little bit of clipping. I put on my most presentable set of clothes. I packed one change of clothes in the small black holdall and placed my documents and my notebook in it.

One morning the air seemed particularly frosty.

"This is it. I think I should go now," I said to Doc. He nodded and went to fetch Wheels. When he returned Doc said very little to me. Gruffly he shook my hand. "I'll miss you. Please come back," he said before turning his back on me. Stores appeared briefly nearby and gave me a brief wave.

"I'm going now. Please can you drop me in the usual place?" I said to Wheels, but he said nothing and went to start the truck.

By the time I got in the truck there was a line of bears peering. They included the females and the cubs. Max, Oskar and Peter the Great were all there. Juno and Julia were there. Slightly apart from the other bears on the edge of the forest Ivan the Terrible glowered enigmatically from between the trees. I felt as if they were waving me off.

"Hey, bears. I'll be back," I called out. A low moan seemed to emanate from Max and Oskar.

"That's what you say now," said Wheels in apparent response to my comment to the bears.

"I mean it," I said with as much conviction as I could muster.

He did not speak as he drove me to our usual place. There were a few flakes of sleet. The bears would be hibernating very shortly and before long there would be snow.

There were no real "goodbyes" between Wheels and me. He just left me, and I trudged towards the town as if I was just going shopping. I headed for a non-descript chain hotel which sat just next to the supermarket. I booked a room for a week, wondering if this was too long. The receptionist gave me an odd look but processed my card payment. When I reached my room and glanced at my reflection in the mirror, I could see why she gave me an odd look. My hair and beard were a mess. I had a gaunt appearance, and my complexion could best be described as grossly weather beaten. My clothing made me look like a tramp as I had an odd mishmash of garments.

I was able to book a flight at the regional airport for the end of the week with the help of the receptionist who kindly printed out the flight ticket. I spent the next few days trying to make myself look more presentable. I visited a barber. I bought some leather town shoes, some smart trousers, a collared shirt and good quality sweater. I also purchased a long, smart overcoat and a Homberg style hat. I stoked up on food at the hotel's breakfast bar and ate further meals at the supermarket cafeteria. I watched the news channel in my hotel room and brought myself up to date with world events, lamentable as they were.

The day came when I took a taxi to the regional airport. No-one batted an eyelid at me. I was just some middle-aged man off to catch a plane. The hat came off for security, but I muffled myself in my hat and coat for much of the time.

My plans for the immediate future somewhat depended on what reception I got from Lizabetta. If she did not want to know me, then as soon as there was a thaw, I would return to Bearswood End on my own.

While I waited for my plane at the regional airport, I brought the diary account in my notebook up to date. It might be my last chance to do so for a while for I had a long journey ahead of me which included more than one flight. It was my dearest wish to return to the bears and I did not want them discovered. However, I was keen for it to be recognised that these bears were truly remarkable.

It was at this point the diary came to an end. There were a few sketches of bears which followed. The book had included many sketches, but these ones appeared to have been drawn from memory since they depicted events at different times. There were also drawings of what I assumed was the village and some men who I believed were Doc, Wheels, and Stores. There was also a sketch of a woman, but it was too badly water stained for me to use when I transcribed the book, as were many other drawings. I assume the scientist had drawn Lizabetta from memory in the hope of seeing her again soon.

Doc's House

I t took me months to transcribe the diary. I had a life to live and a career to pursue. I ran a business from home restoring works of art. My husband and I had family to support. There were two young adult children at university. The scientist had spindly black handwriting and would scribble notes up margins. There were some water stains throughout the booklet. The drawings which had survived were a delight. I did a little every day.

It was clear the scientist did not want the location of Bearswood End discovered. There were features in the diary which gave more than a clue to the continent, the country, and the region. If hard pressed I could probably guess two or three candidates for the actual location. I decided to take out all clues from the transcription. I wouldn't even tell my husband where I thought Bearswood End was situated. He was amused by the whole thing, fortunately, and very much an animal lover. We lived in the countryside, after all, with two dogs, three cats, six hens and a donkey.

It was a good thing we had obliging friends at the farm next door who helped us out with our menagerie when we were ever away. The location was not too cut off. The little hamlet of Appleton Daneby was only ten minutes by car from a mainline station which had a fast train service to London. Whilst many thought of the East of England as an area of fens and country bumpkins the reality was that our local town had now become a centre for a new university which complemented its ancient Minster and Roman remains. It was where my husband was a partner in a local firm of Chartered Accountants.

One April day my business took me to London. I was looking at the magazine rack at the station bookstore while waiting for the train. Normally I did not buy magazines. On this occasion I had time to kill and having decided the newspapers were all too depressing I happened on the nature magazine section. I picked up a glossy publication which looked enticing called 'Popular nature and Geography'. It said it was a fortnightly periodical 'including articles for and about naturalists'. There was a photograph of some Black bears on the front cover. I decided to buy it.

It was an absorbing read and my journey to London passed quickly. As we approached the London terminus, I started to look at a section headed 'News of the Scientific Community'. It had not been a section which had drawn my attention earlier, but I had looked at most of the rest of the magazine. There were a number of sections about conservation projects and the scientists leading them. There was an article about an Oxford professor who had turned his attic into a bat sanctuary. There was then a section with a blurred photograph headed 'Where is the missing professor?'

I recognised the man in the photograph. It was the man who, months ago, had given me the diary in Schiphol Airport. A short paragraph described him as a world-renowned expert on bears and mentioned how the university where he used to have a Chair was concerned about his welfare. It went on to read:

'*The Professor went off on his own to do a solo project which he would not discuss. He failed to return by the due date from his sabbatical. He then appeared many weeks later but only long enough to hand in his resignation. It appears he left his address and put the property up for sale. All he would tell the University before he disappeared was that he was off to start a new life*'.

When the train stopped at the London Terminus I sat there for several minutes. Eventually I was disturbed by the train guard saying,

"Are you alright, madam?"

I grabbed my possessions, mumbled something and hurriedly disembarked from the carriage.

The article distracted me all day. When I got home, I decided to discuss the options with my husband. Duncan is a very practical man, no doubt getting his practicality and dry sense of humour from his Scottish father. On the one hand the university was obviously concerned about the scientist; on the other hand, the scientist wanted to keep Bearswood End secret. After considering my husband's advice, I contacted the university concerned and told them of my meeting in the airport. We had some initial back and forth emails. I let them have excerpts from the diary but nothing which would hint at the location of Bearswood End. I received a message from the Dean about two weeks later. He was very grateful. He asked if he could publish the extracts. He would give me credit for transcribing them.

I mulled over the issue of letting the extracts be published for quite a few days. In the end after receiving a reminder from the Dean I decided that the world should know that the scientist was still working with bears. I double checked that there was no hint about the whereabouts of Bearswood End.

About six weeks later I received a copy of 'Popular Nature and Geography', in the post. There was a short update about the scientist with the extracts I had sent '*With thanks to Mrs Ursula Mathan of Appleton Daneby, UK*'.

I suppose I thought that the episode with the magazine brought matters to a close. Duncan and I went off on a holiday to the West Highlands and enjoyed a couple of weeks visiting Oban and the Isle of Mull. One of our children joined us. She was writing a dissertation on how tourism could help nature if correctly managed, so it was a good excuse to visit the seal sanctuary. Our son was off on military exercises with the University Officer Training Corps.

When we got home, I helped both our children pack up to return to their respective universities. The matter of Bearswood End and the scientist went quite out of my head.

In late October I was checking the spam box of my business email address as I do from time to time. My business has its own website and an email address which often attracts unsolicited advertising. I was actually checking if an email from a client had gone into spam. But I found the following email:

'*Dear Ursula Mathan*

Are you the lady who took custody of a notebook at Schiphol? If so, you have my thanks.

Regards

The Scientist who wrote the diary'

In some ways, it was an oddly worded email. I assumed the scientist had found my website on the internet. There cannot be many Ursula Mathans, let alone ones from Appleton Daneby. However, he was doubtless being careful in case he got the wrong person. So, I replied,

'Dear Scientist

Yes, I am the person you met at Schiphol. You did very well to contact me. I assume you saw the piece in the magazine. I hope it was alright for me to release those excerpts. I was careful not to identify Bearswood End's location. I have worked out in which region you are and have narrowed it down to a couple of places, but I will never give that information away. I am glad you are alright and would be pleased to hear more as to how you and the bears are doing.

Yours sincerely

Ursula Mathan'

I had no reply or so I thought. I speculated to Duncan who I told of the email traffic that either the scientist did not want to reply, or the village was deep in snow so he could not reach the outside world. As it turned the latter was fairly accurate. About three weeks later I received the following email,

'Dear Ursula

I am grateful to you. I never thought anyone could guess the location. This email will be brief since I am relying on our recently obtained satellite dish during a lull in the winter snow. Your name is hugely ironic. 'Ursula' is derived from the Latin for bear. 'Mathan' is, I believe, the Gaelic for bear. I will continue our correspondence in the spring when I have better access to the internet.

Your friend the scientist'

I looked up the meaning of my names. He was correct. My parents had certainly not chosen 'Ursula' because of its meaning. I understood I had been named after my maternal grandmother. My maiden name, Dovebarr was derived from my family's Jewish ancestors. I understood it had been 'Dovber'. My forebears had lived in the forests of Latvia but had settled in England in about 1912. My maternal family had not practiced their ancestral religion apart from the Canadian branch of the family. Like many families of Jewish origin events such as the Russian Revolution and the persecution by the Nazis and World War Two had spread us all over the world. I did not know Hebrew or Yiddish. I really had not researched much about my name. I was very surprised when I now discovered that 'Dovber' could be interpreted as 'Bear bear'.

I told Duncan all about it and asked him about his surname. He too had not realised his surname meant 'bear'.

"It seems to me," said Duncan, "that you are somehow fated to have this connection with bears."

I agreed. I said, "I don't want to find the scientist, however, I think I must be the guardian of the secret of Bearswood End and his work."

Duncan smiled. He said jokingly, "We can always go on a holiday and see other bears than these Brown bears. Maybe Polar or Black bears?"

An idea took hold of me. In July next year I would celebrate my fiftieth birthday. I had cousins in Canada I had never visited in their home city of Toronto. Indeed, I had met them only four times, twice as a child when their parents brought them to England and twice as an adult. They had come to England as students and stayed with my parents for a month. After I had married Duncan, we had gone on a quick tour of some eastern North American cities taking in Boston and Ottawa and Niagara Falls. In Ottawa we spent a day with my cousins and their families. Jo lived with her husband Ira, who was a rabbi, and they had a large number of children. Janice on the other hand was rather 'new age'. She had a pottery and dance studio where she lived with Donna; it was not clear if they were friends or in a relationship and I did not ask. At times Donna would spend time making clay sculptures amongst First Nations' people.

Janice and Jo had travelled to Ottawa especially to meet us.

After our Canadian visit I recall saying to Duncan that we should return and explore more of Canada. There were bears in Canada and while I did not envisage going on some expedition like the scientist, maybe I might be lucky enough to see a bear. A few days later I said to Duncan,

"I want to run away to Canada for my fiftieth birthday."

"Are you chasing after your scientist?" he asked with a smile.

"If he is in Canada, I wouldn't say so to anyone, even you… No, I want to visit Jo and Janice in Toronto and then maybe see just a bit of the country. Can we manage two weeks away? Would that be alright?"

"If that is where you want to go," said Duncan. "Perhaps planning a trip might stop you fretting over the scientist and our weird connection with bears."

Over the next few weeks, I took great pleasure in organising our trip to Canada. Jo and Janice were clearly thrilled that we would visit Toronto. Initially I had a romantic idea that we would simply drive out to some wild place halfway across Canada but when I looked at the distances it did not seem practical in the timescale. So, I looked for somewhere just an hour or two by plane from Toronto. I decided upon Thunder Bay. I had considered going to Vancouver but that would mean a much longer flight. My cousins thought I had made an odd choice, but Duncan decided to leave the choice to me.

Part 2

Bearswood End (2)

The Correspondence

Spring came and eventually a further email from the scientist appeared in my inbox.

'Dear Ursula

I apologise for the brevity of my last email. Communications are difficult for me as you can imagine. The winter conditions are a challenge. I am pleased to tell you that bears, and humans are all doing well. You have my grateful thanks for how you have treated my diary and the information you have in your possession. As you know I was on my way to find Lizabetta when I met you. I was feeling rather low and uncertain of what she would say. I noted you were interested in bears and so I really handed over my notes in a sudden impulse. For some reason I thought someone should know my story.

I thought you would like to know that five cubs were born over the winter and four are doing very well. You may recall Juno had taken up with Ivan the Terrible but became wounded. Despite her adventures she gave birth to two healthy cubs. Alice has had another cub. You may remember she had Una already. Julia had two cubs but unfortunately one died.

The cub was always rather frail. Julia went a little way out of the village and unfortunately the cubs followed. Julia must have been climbing amongst tree roots and loose rocks. There appeared to have been a slight rockfall. Some debris fell on the cub.

When Wheels and Stores found him, he certainly was not covered in debris, and they could not see any overt injuries. Julia and the other cub must have sat with him all night but sadly he was dead. I do wonder if the shock killed him. They persuaded Julia and the other cub who we have called 'Rocky' to return. I called him Rocky since he is very much a survivor.

I have taken the liberty of calling Alice's cub 'Ursula'. I hope you don't mind. Juno's cubs are respectively Borodin and Mussorgsky. Ivan the Terrible is thankfully leaving his family alone at the moment. He is more interested in hunting in the forest.

Well once again, you have my thanks. I hope your own family is well and life is treating you kindly.

Kind Regards

Your friend the scientist'

I replied,

'My friend the Scientist,

Thank you for your email. It is good to know about the cubs. My husband and I are both well. We have been working at our businesses and spending time with our children when they come home.

We have adult children at university. Our youngest Alexander is studying law and has several more years of study. Our oldest Katerina shares your interests. She is just concluding a BSc in Biology and Ecology and then intends to do a Master's degree. My husband is a

Chartered Accountant and as you may know I have a business in fine art restorations.

My husband's interests include Scottish history, whiskey tasting, our garden and travel. Obviously, I am interested in art, but I share Duncan's interest in the garden, and I like knowing about different parts of the world. Like yourself I enjoy sketching.

Duncan and I both like to travel. This summer we are visiting my cousins in Toronto and then going out to Thunder Bay. I want to see Lake Superior and the scenery in that area, and maybe I'll get lucky and get to see some wildlife.

Your communication does not say how it went with Lizabetta. Can I be nosy and ask you if you found her and whether she welcomed your return?

Please do keep in touch. I will never disclose the whereabouts of Bearswood End, even to Duncan, unless you ask me to do so, although Duncan assures me that he would not disclose your secret either.

Your friend

Ursula Mathan'

The answer came speedily. I know not if it was the use of satellite internet which enabled the scientist to reply or whether he went into the town and visited the internet café.

'Dear Ursula

I have spoken to Lizabetta, and she agrees that you should know what happened after I met you at the airport.

When we met, I had left Bearswood End and was on the way to find her. I was very apprehensive. I had no idea how she would react, but I persevered and took the flights which brought me to her home city.

Only when I had arrived at the airport did I try to contact her. At first my phone call went to voicemail. I made a second call when on *the airport bus into the city. Not surprisingly the call started with her sounding taken aback that I was in touch. She expressed astonishment when I told her where I was.*

I fully expected Lizabetta to tell me she did not want to see me. Instead, she gave me directions to her home. Both her parents were now deceased, and she lived on her own. I already knew she worked at the local university and was an expert on eagles.

When she opened the front door of her house it was as if all the years had slipped away. I will not relate our conversations since they are private and personal. Suffice it to say I did tell her my full story, including the whereabouts of Bearswood End.

We spent several weeks together. Lizabetta then agreed to come with me when I returned to Bearswood End. I left for a couple of weeks to go and settle my affairs. I resigned my Chair at the university and gave power of attorney to a lawyer to sell my house and send the proceeds to an account I knew I could access. The proceeds plus my savings would be accessible if the bears needed anything.

Lizabetta similarly settled her affairs. She took a year's sabbatical from her university (she has since resigned) and let her house out to a local family. She gave authority to deal with her affairs to an uncle but said nothing about where she was going. He assumed I think that she was off on a university project. They were not that close.

By the time it was spring I was ready to introduce Lizabetta to Bearswood End. We flew to another area from where we would make our journey by road. We did not wish to attract too much attention. Instead of hiring a vehicle we purchased one. We loaded it up with equipment including a dish for a satellite connection with the internet, more solar panels and a further generator and more medical supplies. There were tools, warm clothing and bedding, waterproof sheeting, a couple of empty plastic barrels and jerry cans we later filled with fuel.

I had kept in touch with Doc by text. Lizabetta and I spent a couple of nights in the hotel near the supermarket and the day then arrived when we met Wheels in the grove of trees by the river. I think originally, I thought Wheels might pick us up, but we had bought so much equipment it was easier just to follow him. The vehicle would prove useful too. Wheels must have set out in the dark because we met him at 5. 30am. We carefully followed him back along the secret trails. All the time we checked that we were not attracting attention.

So, I brought Lizabetta home to Bearswood End. At first, I worried she might not stay but she has spent a winter here and it has not deterred her. We are happy together. The bears have taken to her.

Initially we stayed with Doc, but now we have taken over what was previously a derelict house. We have repaired it, including the chimney. It has a working wood stove and range. We have used what we can to make it as comfortable as possible. Lizabetta has even planted out a little vegetable patch just outside the front door.

The bears have very much taken to her, particularly Peter the Great. They play a little game together. She will roll an item of food to him, say a bread roll or a root vegetable. He will pretend not to catch it. Then he will grab it and roll over on his back tossing the item about with his front paws. It is truly comical to see. When Lizabetta first went up to the ridge to see some eagles Peter insisted on coming with us. To give him his due it did give us a feeling of security to have him as a kind of guard and he kept very quiet when she was watching the birds. She now has a hide constructed and each time she goes to it Peter quietly goes with her. I think he may stop this when he takes up with one of the female bears if he is thinking of mating.

Doc, Wheels and Stores are their usual selves. They have accepted Lizabetta, and she has shown respect and understanding to them. Max and Oskar clearly see her as a friend too. They sit next to her vegetable garden as she weeds it. She has put a token little wooden fence around the patch which a bear could easily trample down, yet they leave it alone and push the cubs away if they try to go into it.

We rarely go to the town these days. Lizabetta has gone there only twice in the last year. We try to be as self-sufficient as we can. The further equipment helps. We obviously did stock up prior to last winter. Our main concern is that of being discovered and of hunters. The logging activity near the settlement has decreased for now since I think they are waiting for certain forest areas to regrow. Two men came near the ridge in the winter, when there had been an unexpected thaw. I am hopeful their hunting trip was not that fruitful as they left quickly and did not return. I also hope these thaws in the winter will not happen too often as the wintry conditions tend to deter visitors.

Lizabetta was initially interested in publishing her research on the eagles, but now she agrees we need to keep Bearswood End a secret. I was very lucky my notebook fell into your hands. I am hopeful that Lizabetta will eventually find a way to get her research back to the scientific community without indicating our location. For now, she is content.

I do hope your trip to Thunder Bay is successful. Your daughter may find that area of interest to her.

I wish your husband and your family very well.

Very Best Wishes

Your friend the Scientist'

I resolved I would email the scientist again once we had been on our trip. I smiled at the way he continued to call himself 'the scientist'. I knew who he was, at which university he had been a professor and I had a very good idea from which country and city Lizabetta hailed, but if he preferred this cloak of anonymity who was I to argue?

Duncan and I eventually booked the trip to Toronto and Thunder Bay for the last week in June and the first week in July. We would start in Toronto and then travel on to Thunder Bay. At first Alexander and Katerina were unsure about joining us but in the event, they were both won over. Alexander discovered his university exams would be over and he would just be at a loose end. He had signed up for a mini pupillage shadowing a barrister for two weeks in late July, and then had managed to get himself four weeks work experience at a local solicitors' practice. It seemed he had covered all the bases.

"As long as you pay for everything," he said stretching his long legs over the settee and yawning. "I could do with a holiday," he added as if no-one else needed a break.

Katerina was initially unsure if she wanted to join us but by then she believed her thesis would be finished. She had a new relationship with another student, Daniel. It appeared he reassured her that he would take the opportunity to visit his granny in the Orkney Islands at that time. He suggested they might get together in Edinburgh for a few days on her return and perhaps venture for a couple of days to western Scotland and visit a seal project there. I knew that they intended to do their Master's degrees in the same modules and were very close, but she jumped at the chance to go briefly to Canada once she had made arrangements to meet Daniel afterwards. I think she was keen on spotting some wildlife near Thunder Bay.

We booked an apartment in an 'aparthotel' in northern Toronto for the first few days of our trip. Janice and Jo and Ira lived in nearby suburbs and were several years younger than me. Ira's synagogue was in the same suburb as the hotel. Ira and Jo and his sister Rachel did not live far away. She lived in a condominium town house with her husband Stephen, a dentist, and she worked part-time in a Kosher bakery. As yet, Rachel had no children. Jo and Ira had four little girls, under the age of ten who looked like each other as peas in a pod. Jo did not go out to work but helped out with a Jewish Women's group. Janice seemed a bit of a free spirit. However, I now knew she was living in a happy relationship with Donna. She had her own small business making pottery and handmade cards and worked part-time in her dance studio. Duncan and I had chosen the apartment arrangement both to give Katerina and Alexander some space and also so we could be close to my relations rather than staying in downtown Toronto.

We booked accommodation in a guest house near Thunder Bay. The Comfort Forest Clearing B and B sounded as if it might have some character. It was run by a Barry and Molly Jenkins and was a few miles outside Thunder Bay on the edge of the forest on the strangely named 'Mile Post Road'. I could not wait to get there!

The time came for us to set off on our journey. The airport leg of the journey was very tedious. There were no encounters with mysterious scientists, just a lot of hanging around. I slept for part of the flight but still felt exhausted when we reached Toronto. We were lucky that Janice was able to meet us at the airport and whisk us away to our apartment. She said she would come back later, and we would have a family get-together in a local restaurant.

Toronto had its fair share of tall buildings, and our aparthotel was twelve stories high. Our apartment was on the eighth floor which gave us good views of the locality. It had a small balcony which Duncan and Alexander quickly adopted. They had a view of a railway line and took a strange pleasure in having bets with each other as to the number of cars on the lengthy freight trains.

Over our few days in Toronto, we made the obligatory trip up the CN tower, and we went to the aquarium and to the waterfront. We looked at the shops at the Eaton Centre. Katerina managed to persuade Rachel to take her Jo and the girls to Toronto Zoo, while Duncan, Alexander and I visited the brewery situated in the old railway roundhouse in downtown Toronto and wandered around the railway museum where it is situated. I would have liked to go to the zoo but realised there would have been no room for me in the car. As it was, I found the old roundhouse very atmospheric.

We enjoyed several family meals including one to celebrate my birthday. It was clear to me that our lives were very different, but I was still pleased as to how well we got on despite our differences. Ira, Jo and Rachel were hugely keen on maintaining all cultural and religious Jewish roots whereas I was never religious and just accepted my ancestry was a facet of who I was. The other side of the coin was Janice, who as far as I could tell was not rooted to any culture or way of life. It seemed she had tried Judaism, Catholicism and Buddhism in succession. She was clearly artistic and seemed most content when talking about her pottery and handmade greeting card business.

The day came to fly off to Thunder Bay. We said our "Goodbyes" since on the return journey we would simply have a layover for a few hours to change planes in Toronto before flying back to England.

The flight to Thunder Bay was not particularly long, and it was quite a speedy process to get out of the airport and pick up our hire car. Fortunately, my husband Duncan was well used to driving different hire vehicles in different locations on our foreign holidays. The car was large and comfortable, so we soon found ourselves on the outskirts of the city of Thunder Bay. We then picked our way on what appeared to be a road towards the mountains and wilderness. Before long we found Mile Post Road which appeared to be an unmetalled track. Just a few hundred metres up it was a sign pointing along another track. That was the sign to the guest house. Thankfully that piece of track was quite short as it was narrow with a sign partway along saying 'moose crossing'.

Barry and Molly Jenkins came to the door to greet us. Barry had a shock of white hair and seemed rather older than Molly a slim, lively, middle-aged figure. The house was set in a forest clearing which was now a lawned garden. In front of the house was a gravelled parking area. The lower level of the house which incorporated a basement was built of brick, while the upper level was built of wood, painted white. There was a tiled roof. There were half a dozen steps up to the front door. A balcony terrace ran along the back of the house at a similar level to the front door, several feet above ground level. We received a friendly greeting from our hosts who sat us down for coffee and tea in the spacious residents' lounge before showing us to our rooms.

Barry had recently retired from a construction business he used to run with his son while Molly cheerfully spoke of her other occupation which was as a part-time magician performing tricks at children's parties. They gave us plenty of local information and seemed eager to please and interested in our interests. As Molly was showing us to our rooms she said,

"Now be sure to keep the downstairs doors and windows closed. We don't want any bears getting in the house."

I thought this was a jokey way of reminding us about security.

Over the next few days, we explored the area quite extensively. The first attraction we visited was the Fort William Historical Park which was a reconstruction of an old fort. It was all very well done but maybe I just was not in the right mood. The people doing displays in the park wore historical dress and always stayed in character. When I stopped to ask the way to the toilets, I was not in the right frame of mind for the conversation which followed,

"Have you travelled far?" I was asked as I stood uncomfortably wanting to find the ladies' toilets sooner rather than later.

To which I answered, "From Britain," and got a reply, "Did you come in a big canoe?"

My response may have sounded terse. "No on a plane. Please where are the toilets?"

My mood improved as we continued our exploration over the next few days. The area seemed a hidden gem.

We had a drive out to the beginning of the Sleeping Giant Provincial Park which juts out into the waters of Lake Superior. The sun shone and the lake looked serene, and the scenery was spectacular. We did not venture too far into the park, not being equipped for camping and wanting to search for some dinner at one of Thunder Bay's restaurants. We also ventured to Ouimet Canyon

Provincial Park and took a walk to a viewing platform to admire the spectacular views which have been compared with the Grand Canyon. Certainly, this rugged canyon has dizzying views if you look down it, and it also has a reputation for a different microclimate on the floor of the canyon than at the top of it. I could tell that both Katerina and Alexander were impressed.

One very sunny morning we visited the Kakabeca Falls. A boardwalk wraps its way around the falls which at forty metres high in many ways rivals Niagara Falls, since the setting is more natural. Breath-taking as it was the falls left us with a taste for more exploration. So, we drove further and eventually found ourselves on a lonely road following the Pigeon River close to the US border. Now and again, we spotted a clearing with a trailer parked in it or a shack, and a sign saying, 'Trespassers keep out' or 'No trespassers'. We saw no vehicle for miles.

Suddenly there was a huge flapping of wings, and a massive bird nearly struck the bonnet of the car.

"An eagle," said Alexander in awe as it flew away. "What can beat that?"

He might well have asked as not twenty minutes later a moose lumbered across the lonely road. Duncan braked to let it go and Katerina cursed she was just seconds too late in efforts to photograph it. There was, however, a broad smile on her face.

Our few days in Thunder Bay were drawing to a close. Tomorrow would be the penultimate full day, so we took ourselves to one of the best restaurants in downtown Thunder Bay for a nice dinner. As we sat at the table Katerina said,

"This has been a superb trip even if we have not seen any bears."

We all agreed and expressed regret at the brevity of our trip. Local information indicated there were Black bears in the area, sometimes coming into areas where there were people. We had seen deer more than once and of course the moose and the eagle. White tailed deer, Black bears, moose, wolves and lynx were all known to be common in the area, but some were easier to see than others.

Next morning, we were a little slow getting going, after all we were nearing the end of our trip. Molly served breakfast until 9.30 so Duncan and I hoped to appear about twenty past, and we were leaving it to Katerina and Alexander to decide if they would get up for breakfast at all. About half past eight there was a hammering on our door, and I could hear Molly saying,

"Ursula, Duncan... come quick there is a bear in the garden!"

Duncan jumped out of the shower. We both threw some clothes on. We could hear Molly knocking on Katerina and Alexander's doors. I could hear Katerina say keenly, "I'm coming, I'm coming."

Of Alexander there was no response. I poked my head around the door of his room, and he muttered something about, "Too tired, enjoy your bear, Mother." I left him to sleep.

Duncan, Katerina, and I hastened downstairs to the residents' sitting room which had patio doors which normally opened onto the veranda.

"Keep the doors and windows closed," hissed Molly. "He's a young Black bear. I do hope he won't try to break into the basement. I think it's secure but there is always a risk."

I nodded and peered out of the window. A face popped up from below the balcony and a couple of beady eyes seemed to be returning my gaze. The young Black bear must have been standing on his hind quarters to look over the top of the veranda. The face disappeared only to reappear at the other end of the terrace about half a minute later.

"He's beautiful," said Katerina, clearly captivated.

Molly said, "I believe he is quite young, possibly a male kicked out by his mom."

The bear moved away from the veranda and started to explore the garden. First, he took a drink from a little pond. Then he knocked over a deckchair which had been left out and examined it. The garden had some hanging baskets bedecked with flowers hanging from a few of the tree branches. The young Black bear stood up as he approached one and pinged it with his paw, so the basket rocked back and forth. He did this several times to each of the baskets. Katerina was agog with excitement and whispered,

"Why, he's just like a child playing."

Duncan was busily photographing the bear. I could see how dark the bear's coat was. He had a light area of fur just around the nose. When he was on all fours, he did not look particularly tall. This was in marked contrast to when he stood up.

After a few more minutes the bear started sniffing around the garden flowers. Evidently, they were not of interest. He peered back at the house and stood there staring for about half a minute. After that he headed towards the forest and disappeared behind the trees. He was gone.

The trip to Thunder Bay seemed to have a profound effect on all of us. Duncan and I were more reflective about our working lives and began to seriously consider plans for retirement in a few years' time. We had a small disused brick barn adjacent to our house and we began the process of converting it into a holiday cottage.

Katerina could not get enough of bears. Once she had her Master's degree Daniel and her involved themselves mainly in various UK mammal conservation projects working towards their Doctorates, but she would frequently wistfully talk about going to work with bears overseas if she ever got the chance.

Alexander was probably the least affected, although he said the Thunder Bay trip was the best family holiday he had ever had. He knuckled down to his legal work and in due course became a successful barrister. His Chambers appeared to be full of dynamic and successful people. Not so long ago a member of his Chambers had become a Member of Parliament for a constituency in northern England and had then risen to be leader of the opposition and was now Prime Minister.

A few years past. Alexander married another young lawyer, and they recently had our first grandchild Iris. They lived about sixty miles away, so we saw them from time to time. Duncan only worked part-time at accountancy now and the holiday cottage was very popular with travellers. Katerina and Daniel disappeared for months at a time on projects in remote places. Once they were thrilled to work with Polar bears in the Arctic for two months. Mostly they seem to end up on remote Scottish islands or in Scandinavia undertaking projects on seals.

The email correspondence with the scientist settled down to twice yearly. I loved to read how the bears were getting on. In a way I felt I knew them. They seemed to be thriving although inevitably there was the occasional death. When I heard about such a tragedy it felt like hearing of the death of a distant relative.

The world was not getting any easier for people. I liked to think of Bearswood End tucked away from many bad things, but I worried how the ills of the outside world might potentially impinge on the village of the bears. I hoped all the residents would remain safe in their secret place. I knew there was to be an international conference soon on nature, but I had little faith that it would protect places like Bearswood End. These international affairs seemed to get hi-jacked by people with their own agendas, be it politicians trying to make themselves popular or campaigners wishing to promote the cause of the moment. Our own new Prime Minister was set to attend and would be looking for a soundbite.

One day I received an email from the scientist which quite disturbed me.

'*Dear Ursula*

I hope you and the family are well. I am aware from my brief contacts with the outside world it is a difficult and challenging place. Unfortunately, we have our troubles too in Bearswood End.

First, I have to report some sad news amongst the bears. Over the last year I had noticed that Max the bear was slowing down considerably. His movements seemed stiff, and he barely left the village. Recently he showed a reduced appetite. He then retired to his den and after a short illness he died. The reality is that he was an old bear who might not have lived so long without the support of the village. We were all very upset and it was no mean feat burying him. There is now a cairn of stones and Stores has carved out a wooden plaque with his name on it.

Oskar, who is I, think a little younger was initially bereft and actually sat by the cairn for two days. However, he has now taken up with a young half-grown bear Jeremy and seems to be guiding him in things like how to drive one of our adapted vehicles. It is quite touching to see.

On the human side we have our troubles. None of us are getting any younger. Doc is troubled with arthritis. Most worryingly Wheels has eye issues. Doc, believing he has cataracts, sent him off to town. Wheels pretended to be a tourist and managed somehow to get an eye examination which confirmed Doc's fears. There will therefore come a point when he will have to leave the village for a while. He says he will go to his hometown. Stores may want to go with him. They will pretend to have been away travelling. I am not looking forward to their absence although I am sure they will return.

And matters get worse; you must have read there is to be a large conference on world nature sponsored by the UN. A large part of the conference is in Geneva, but it is to have an 'away leg' in an area of outstanding natural interest. It has just been announced this will take place over four days in the town in the valley below us. What it says online is "delegates will be taken to explore nearby wildlife by young academic volunteers". I am terrified they will come up to the settlement and might find our village.

This is all due to happen at the worst possible time, with Wheels and Stores likely to be away. Wheels has talked of delaying his treatment but Doc says medically that could be harmful so I think he should get on with it. His eyesight is too important.

Ursula, we need your help. You have mentioned your daughter's scientific work. If you think she can be trusted (please don't take that the wrong way) please could you tell her my full story? She can read the diary and you can tell her where you think we are; your knowledge is pretty accurate. Then could you ask her to find someone, a younger person, who might join us for a while? She would need to make sure they were trustworthy and that they would not give away our location. I am sure the bears would not mind if it was a couple, but as we are getting older, we could do with some younger human residents, even if it was only for some months. It would be a plus if she could get herself involved in the conference somehow and keep us informed.

I have consulted with Lizabetta, Doc, and Wheels and Stores before sending you this email. I do not send it lightly and I apologise if it puts you in any difficulties.

With very best wishes

Your friend the Scientist'

I read the email several times and went and sat outside our house in the garden to think.

A voice interrupted my thoughts.

"There you are," said Duncan. "You look serious."

I told him about the email and said,

"It is not a question of whether Katerina can be trusted. I am sure Katerina and Daniel can both be trusted. It is more they will want to go themselves."

"Isn't that what the scientist intended?" said Duncan. I nodded in the affirmative.

"Would it be so bad?" he went on. "They disappear into the wilds half the time anyway."

I was surprised by his answer but saw the logic of it. I could see Katerina and Daniel making a life off-grid. If they ever had a family, I was sure they would cope somehow. They were intelligent and resourceful young people. The international conferences' away leg presented a bigger challenge.

I sent an acknowledgement to the scientist. About two weeks later Katerina and Daniel made one of their rare visits. For the first time I told Katerina everything and let her read the full transcription of the diary with Daniel. As I had done, they went to sit in the garden to think. I could see them earnestly talking. They sat there for about two hours.

Daniel Campbell was a studious and thoughtful young man. Apart from an old grandmother he had few relatives and seemed to have adopted my family as his own. His parents had died in a plane crash when he was 14 but despite this he had shone academically, being urged on by his grandmother and great-uncle who had been a sheep farmer on a lonely island. He was very practical and seemed very at ease in wild places. Katerina's heart and soul were devoted to nature, so he seemed to complete her world.

When they came inside Katerina said,

"As it happens, Daniel and I have already been signed up by the university to do some work with the conference and we will try to get signed up for the 'away leg'. Daniel and I are going to Bearswood End after the conference is over, we think. We hope we can get a bit of research funding from our university without disclosing the location at all, and if we cannot get funding we'll go anyway. If it works out, you may not see us for a long time. The difficult part will be to protect Bearswood End and not to alert anyone to its presence."

The statement was not unexpected to Duncan and I. We were both philosophical.

I sent an email to the scientist.

'My dear friend

My daughter Katerina and her boyfriend Daniel will be joining you in Bearswood End before the end of the summer. Look after them please. Before they arrive, they will be involved in the conference and trying to keep everyone away from your village.

Very Best Wishes

Ursula'

The conference was starting quite soon so Katerina and Daniel had little time to prepare. They managed to get themselves signed up for both the Geneva leg and the away section. I kept the scientist informed.

For the away section Katerina and Daniel had been assigned to work with a team of local guides to show the VIPs nature sites. I knew they would familiarise themselves with the geography of the region and try to keep visitors away from Bearswood End somehow. It was this part which worried us all the most. I expressed my worries to Duncan. He replied,

"Katerina and Daniel are intelligent adults. If anyone can protect Bearswood End they can. I propose we leave it to them. We should plan a little trip for ourselves. I suggest we have a tour combining visits of Scottish castles with some of the best distilleries. The castles for you and the whiskey for me!"

I liked the idea very much. Duncan could always make me smile. I tried to think about Scottish castles and not dwell on the worry about Bearswood End.

Part 2

Bearswood End (5)

The Conference

I listened to news programmes, checked online and read newspapers about the forthcoming world nature conference. It appeared it was to be chaired by African academic Dr Godfrey Joseph. He had an impeccable academic record both from studies in Lagos and from work at the University of Cambridge. Katerina had met him several times and told me he was a mesmerising speaker with a special interest in elephants. He was tall and imposing with a smile as wide as his massive chest. The United States of America was to be represented by Senator Brad T Morton Wayney junior. He was a well-known Anglophile who liked to emphasise his Green credentials by pointing out he had a share in a recycling plant in the north of England. The plant was in the constituency of the UK's current Prime Minister, Percy Vere.

Percy Vere had previously practiced as a barrister from the same Chambers as Alexander. With suave good looks he was keen on emphasising his alleged working-class roots. The said roots were slightly dubious, and he had certainly made good from his legal practice. He had the gift of the gab and looked most comfortable on a stage addressing a conference or at a craft beer or real ale pub drinking a pint and giving a little off the cuff press conference. He did not give the appearance of being keen on the outdoors.

The Russian Federation was to be represented by their Minister for Tourism and Natural Resources Konstantin Nikitin and China's representative was to be a Zhao Hou. I had heard nothing of the Chinese representative previously, but I had heard of Helga Thomson the twenty-two-year-old environmental campaigner who was to address the conference.

I listened and read avidly to the news reports of the Geneva leg of the conference. I liked what I read of Dr Joseph's opening address. He said,

"The world is both a precious and dangerous place. There are not enough resources to go round, and man is not always kind to the animal kingdom. We can save the planet but that won't necessarily result in saving animal species. Eco warriors who lie down in the road to protest about fossil fuels do nothing for the animal in the forest being cut down to make wood pellets. The activist who lets out captive animals does not always check if they can survive in the wild. We need a balanced approach. The climate campaigners can do their job, but we need game parks, breeding programmes and protected corridors to protect many species. The breeding programmes at wildlife parks and zoos in the West have their place as long they recognise, that they house wild animals who deserve our respect and are not pets."

The Press picked the story up with a headline 'Game parks, protected corridors and breeding programmes needed'. A picture of a smiling Dr Joseph visiting some elephants in a zoo near Geneva was shown.

Our own Prime Minister, Percy Vere did the inevitable off the cuff press conference drinking a steiner of beer in a Swiss beer garden. He smiled cheerfully to the film crews. His interview was broadcast on the television news. He said,

"I think our country presents a great future. It can give a great future for wildlife and a great future for the working man."

He was pressed by well-known British political reporter Bett Hickett,

"How, Mr Vere? The British people will want to have more detail."

"As I said in Conference," Percy Vere started, "my government will be one of opportunity in particular to the working man. There will also be a range of measures for wildlife."

"What are they?" she persisted. "Prime Minister isn't it true you have no measures, and you are just here to pick up soundbites?"

"Now, Miss Hickett," he responded. "You would not expect me to announce measures in a beer garden, the proper place will be in the House of Commons."

"Is that because you are still making up your policies?" said Bett Hickett rudely, jamming the microphone nearly into Percy Vere's face.

Percy Vere kept his cool.

"Look, Miss Hickett," he smiled, "I've been bullied by better than you. As a working class lad clambering up the legal pole I had to contend with all manner of obstacles. Now if you excuse me, I will finish my drink."

I could not help but be amused by the news report and mentioned it in email traffic to the scientist. He was more interested in Dr Godfrey Joseph's words. He said,

'*I have met Godfrey Joseph several times. We shared similar views about wildlife. I am pleased he has risen to such importance. It's a pity things are so difficult in respect of protecting the bears. On his own I think I might have trusted him. Some of the others worry me. Even that environmentalist girl Helga Thomson concerns me. I dread someone like her discovering the village. She would probably want to bulldoze the houses and banish Doc, Lizabetta, Wheels, Stores and myself.*'

The news media showed Zhao Hou explaining about a Panda conservation project. Konstantin Nikitin gave a short interview to a French reporter. He spoke only in Russian through a translator. The interview was then syndicated across the news media. The gist of his interview was that Russia wished to fully support its wildlife through tourism and that included organised hunting parties. He expressed a particular fondness for bear hunts. My blood ran cold. I emailed Katerina to ask her who was on the away leg of the conference. An answer came back swiftly.

'*All the main delegates I am afraid. Like you I am worried by Mr Nikitin. Daniel and I have currently been assigned respectively to Dr Joseph and Senator Wayney. The Senator seems pleasant enough. He has an adult daughter who runs an animal rescue centre in the north of England. He does not take fools gladly. If he is irritated, he tends to say "goddam" under his breath. I will have to be careful he does not realise I am trying to steer him away from certain areas. However, I am also very concerned about Helga Thomson. She is such an unknown quantity.*'

The time approached for Helga Thomson to make her keynote speech. The news media showed how her supporters had blocked Geneva's roads. About a hundred of them sat on the tarmac outside the conference centre holding banners and placards saying things such as 'Ban cars', 'Destroy Industry',' Save the planet' and 'End fuel use'. Apparently, the delegates had difficulty getting into the conference centre. The news showed Senator Wayney running a gauntlet between shouting protestors to get into the front of the building. He paused at the front door to speak to an interviewer,

"I admire these kids for wanting to save the planet," he said, "but they've got it all wrong. They couldn't demonstrate like this in China or Russia. Also, if we can't save some of our precious animals who is the planet for?"

With that he sped inside. Most of the other delegates went through the back entrance.

All the news channels covered some footage of Helga Thomson. Petite and very blonde she sported a long plait going down her back and a small tattoo on her forehead which said 'earth'. She stood in front of the microphone. The crowd was hushed. She said,

"This conference is a side show… a waste of time and resources. Think how much fossil fuels have been used to get people here including the media and power this conference centre."

She had a point.

"And you are not even talking about the right things. We should not be discussing individual species but how we save the whole planet. We need to stop the use of private cars. We need to stop power stations and factories gushing out filth. We need to stop the planet overheating. You should not be here talking about White rhino or Black rhino breeding programmes. Or what Polar bears will eat when ice melts… or the survival of the great ape…or any of that. Maybe man should not hunt the tiger or the jaguar, but this conference will not save our planet for future generations. My movement is the next generation, and we don't want the things our parents have done. I don't care about the outcome of this conference…"

There was some disquiet from the body of the conference hall. One could here calls of, "Save our animals," and a slow handclap.

Helga Thomson continued,

"I don't care about the outcome of this conference. My supporters and myself want to change government policies in a way which we think will save the planet not just breed a few animals."

She finished her address and was bundled out of the hall, but Bett Hickett managed to catch her in a corridor,

"Miss Thomson, why aren't you demonstrating in China or India or Russia… major users of fossil fuel instead of being dismissive about efforts to save wildlife?"

Helga was hustled up the corridor saying, "This conference is a waste of time. We should not be wasting resources."

"Don't you want animals to be protected?" pressed Miss Hickett obviously followed by her cameraman.

"I don't care about this wildlife conference," said Helga as she was bundled into a waiting limousine.

The tabloid newspapers and online blogs had a field-day. Headlines abounded such as 'Helga does not care about wildlife', and 'Environmentalist who wants to stop cars leaves by car'. There were reports showing Helga's picture with a long nose superimposed on it, saying 'Helga's true face' .

A few publications did go with Helga's suggestion that the conference was a bit of a side-show. While I did not agree with Helga Thomson, I thought some newspaper articles went too far. I also felt the wildlife conference had turned into a media circus with politicians trying to get the best soundbite. Katerina agreed with me when I emailed her to get confirmation of who was going on the away leg of the conference.

It appeared that the main 'delegates' on this part of the conference were to be Dr Godfrey Joseph, Senator Brad T Morton Wayney junior and Konstantin Nikitin. Zhao Hou, Percy Vere and Helga Thomson were not attending. Helga Thomson had left the conference altogether. Zhao Hou was staying in Geneva. Percy Vere was returning to the UK briefly since there were to be national strikes in the brewing industry at home, but he would return for the end of the conference.

Katerina was worried about Konstantin Nikitin's intentions. With all the spotlight on Helga Thomson, the issue of Konstantin Nikitin's support of hunting had made surprisingly little news. The UK news media had recently turned their attention to the national brewery workers' strike and how our beer loving barrister Prime Minister who emphasised his working-class roots would cope with it. Even some time after the conference no-one mentions the away leg, so I feel it worthwhile to omit the location from this narrative to further protect Bearswood End.

I emailed the scientist,

'Katerina and Daniel will do their best to keep people away from Bearswood End. But you must keep a low profile. The bears need to stay close.'

The scientist responded,

'At the moment, the only humans are Doc, Lizabetta and myself. Wheels and Stores have gone away so Wheels can have some preliminary treatment to his eyes. Oskar, Peter the Great and Ivan the Terrible have slowed down a great deal. Juno, Julia, and Jeremy are active although Juno and Julia tend to stick to where they have their cubs. I know there is still a hunting camp below the settlement. I hope

Nikitin does not go on a hunting expedition. Please pass on my contact details such as they are to Katerina, and please could I have her contact details?'

Katerina was only too pleased to be in direct touch with the scientist. I knew the next few days would be very difficult but there was nothing I could do myself. I waited at home with Duncan for news.

Part 2
Bearswood End (6)
The Away Trip

I have tried to think hard how I would describe what happened next. I wasn't there so obviously this is not a first-hand account. I have pieced together the events from accounts from the scientist, Katerina, Daniel, and a few Press statements so as to make it into a coherent narrative.

Those taking part in the 'away leg' of the conference flew off to the regional airport nearest the town in the valley. The trip was intended to only last four days but because there were high profile delegates, they were placed in the area's most luxurious hotel a few miles down the valley. Those working on the conference including Katerina and Daniel found themselves in small hotels and guest houses around the town. There was an introductory meeting next day at the hotel. Local guides were proposing to take the delegates for nature trails along the river valley and to a sanctuary for the region's birds of prey where they could meet eagles being re-habilitated to go back in the wild.

Senator Wayney and Dr Joseph seemed enthusiastic about the programme. The Senator said,

"I'm all for animal sanctuaries. My daughter Penny rescues domestic and farm animals in England. I know it's not the same, but I support the concept."

Dr Godfrey was all smiles, but Konstantin Nikitin just scowled at everyone.

Up at Bearswood End there were not fires. Dwellings and tracks had been disguised. The scientist and Doc tried to encourage the bears to stay around the village by offering as much tasty food as they could lay their hands upon.

The delegates were taken with their staff to the sanctuary for the birds of prey and Dr Joseph and the Senator seemed to thoroughly enjoy their time there. Konstantin Nikitin walked around scowling with his hands in his pockets. He had come there in a separate vehicle which Katerina assumed he had hired rather than in the conference minibus. He was accompanied by his security detail which consisted of two 'heavies' clad in black suits. The three men kept whispering to each other in Russian.

A buffet lunch had been laid on in a refreshment area and when Katerina and Daniel went to escort delegates there Nikitin said,

"I am leaving shortly to go on a bear hunt."

The colour drained from Katerina's face.

"That's not on the programme," she said, "and it's hardly helping the wildlife."

"In my country," said Nikitin, "the two are not seen as incompatible. This little excursion is for children, and I am now off to be a grown-up."

She tried to press him further to stay but he was having none of it.

"At least please tell the organisers where you are going, if only for security."

With apparent reluctance Nikitin told her his destination which transpired to be the hunting camp below the settlement. Soon he sped off in a black SUV with smoked glass in the windows accompanied by his heavies.

Katerina pulled Daniel to one side.

"Communications don't always work up at Bearswood End. I must try and find my way there and warn them," she said. "I will send messages, but I need to get there by tonight. I don't think Nikitin will go hunting today. He also must get to the hunting camp."

Daniel nodded. "But how are you going to get there?"

"Get where?" Dr Joseph appeared and interjected. "What are you up to 'senior student'?" That was his nickname for her.

Katerina replied, "Mr Nikitin and his security detail have left us and are going to a hunting camp to go on a bear hunt. I want to contact some wildlife preservationists who are a bit off-grid to warn them... since it may affect their projects."

It was almost the truth.

Dr Joseph said,

"Daniel, please take Katerina in the minibus to the car hire depot. Katerina use the conference card to get a vehicle. Daniel, please come straight back since we will need the minibus to get back to the hotel. Everyone is enjoying lunch here, so they won't notice if you are gone a while." He turned to Katerina,

"Senior student. Do take care."

Katerina and Daniel thanked him profusely. Then they hurried on their way.

Katerina hired a sturdy small off-road vehicle. She drove away from the town and crossed the river. She pulled off the road by the river and attempted to send more messages to the scientist. She had details of where Bearswood End lay for emergency purposes which she had memorised, but she had never envisaged going there on her own. So having sent her messages she felt no option but to press onwards. She headed for the mountains, first passing a few isolated farms and the entrance to the hunting camp. Eventually she reached the settlement where the scientist had started his adventure. She stopped at the bar and ordered a small beer to parch her thirst. The barman asked where she was going, and she vaguely mentioned about conservation work. She took the opportunity to ask if any hunters had passed through the settlement. He told her that no-one had been this way recently but,

"I do hear they are planning on going hunting for bear at first light. Rumour has it they are going up beyond the loggers. No-one local will go that way… terrain is too dangerous… folk from outside who go that way never come back. A naturalist disappeared some years ago. He was never seen again… They would be better going down to the river valley… safer."

He paused. "You are not thinking of going that way?"

Katrina lied in reply, "Of course not."

She drove downhill a short way when she left in case she was watched and then turned around and sped past the bar. She left the settlement behind and carried on past the loggers. Eventually she reached a clearing where there were piles of brushwood and fallen trees heaped. She knew these covered the way to a hidden trail. She parked her vehicle and covered it in brushwood and then searched for the trail. Time was marching on, and she wanted to be at the village before nightfall.

She had been trudging along a track which did have a few tyre marks for a good forty minutes when she heard and saw a rather battered truck coming towards her. She froze in her tracks. Was it hunters? It slowed down and as it stopped, she saw that there was a bear in the driving seat and a man in the passenger seat. A thin man got out and smiled,

"Katerina, I presume!" he said. "Oskar and I came to find you after I got your messages. Suggest you clamber in the back. Lizabetta will find you something to eat in our house and you can bed down for the night."

"Thank you," said Katerina. "I think we may have to plan what to do at first light since hunters are coming this way."

She clambered in the back not thinking twice about being driven by a bear.

Later that day as it became dusk, back at the hotel Dr Joseph was quizzing Daniel about Katerina's whereabouts. Daniel was apprehensive for her safety but did not want to show it. Dr Joseph was very suspicious of his explanations. At first light he crept out of the hotel with the intent of borrowing a car from somewhere and finding Katerina. As he came out of his room and made his way to the lift Dr Joseph stepped in front of him.

"Going somewhere?" he said.

Daniel tried to bluff his way, but it did not work. Finally, he said,

"Katerina is in touch with some people who are helping protect and support a large number of Brown bears in a hidden valley. They do not want their location given away, but the fear is the hunting trip will venture too close to the valley. I have heard nothing from Katerina since last night."

"Come on," said Dr Joseph, "what are we waiting for... I'll drive you? You direct me. I promise not to spill the beans! I am tougher than I look, young man... In Africa I have stood up to ivory hunters."

They took one of the conference delegation vehicles and drove off with the sun yet to fully rise. Before they left Dr Joseph put a small box in the back.

"What's in there?" said Daniel.

"Firecrackers and pepper spray... it was for protection if we were attacked on the planned wildlife walk today. It might do to bother the hunters," said Dr Joseph with a broad grin. "The delegates can have a lie-in instead..."

At first light the hunters also set off. As far as Katerina could understand later most hunters at the camp wanted to go to the river valley but Nikitin and his men wanted to go into the mountains. The result was Nikitin went off with a sole guide and his two 'heavies' in a Jeep towards the mountains, but the rest went to the river valley. They didn't know it, but Dr Joseph and Daniel were only minutes behind them. They also were unaware that the scientist, Doc, Katerina, and Oskar were acting as lookouts.

Daniel only had directions second-hand from Katerina, but they sped through the settlement and passed the loggers bumping along the dirt road. Then they spotted the Jeep marked with the logo of the hunting camp parked in a clearing. They stopped their vehicle and clambered out, not before Dr Joseph had stuffed a few items into his pockets from his box. There appeared to be some boot prints on a trail, so they started to follow that path.

Most of the bears had hunkered down in Bearswood End but there was no telling Ivan the Terrible what to do nor two young bears, Borodin and Mussorgsky. All three had failed to stay in the village and had wandered well away from the lookouts. Katerina was aware of this as the hunters moved ever closer.

Daniel and Dr Joseph trudged up the trail unsure of where they were going when ahead of them, they caught sight of Konstantin Nikitin lying on a rock pointing a large calibre rifle at something. A man who they took to be the guide was also holding a rifle and was crouched beside him. To one side the two 'heavies' were crouched down beside some bushes fingering some handguns. The figure of a bear could just be discerned in Nikitin's line of sight.

Dr Joseph let off a firecracker. A split second later there was a sharp retort from Nikitin's rifle. It seemed clear he had missed since another split second later a huge bear came charging through the undergrowth towards his attackers. The two 'heavies' crashed through the undergrowth and fled. Dr Joseph lobbed a cannister of pepper-dust not at the bear but at his attackers. A waft probably slowed down the bear. The guide took the opportunity to crawl backwards and then fled in the same direction as the 'heavies'. The bear was roaring and standing on his hindquarters. Nikitin had dropped his rifle and was rubbing his eyes and swearing in Russian.

Daniel was aware that the 'heavies' were running towards their vehicle and did not seem aware of Dr Joseph and himself in the confusion. He heard the ignition in the distance and a screech of tyres. Then he heard a voice from an opposite direction,

"Borodin... back off... back off." It was the scientist. Then Daniel heard Katerina's voice,

"Daniel, Dr Joseph... stay where you are. We can see you. You need to let things calm down."

They did as they were bid. After several minutes, the air cleared. Daniel and Dr Joseph edged slowly forward. Katerina and the scientist moved in towards Konstantin Nikitin and Borodin moved back somewhat still roaring. Nikitin made to grab his rifle, but Katerina was just close enough to kick it out of the way. Nikitin was still in prone position and grabbed her ankle and tried to pull her over.

"You bitch, you pigs," and some expletives in Russian he was yelling.

Borodin had backed further away but emerging through the undergrowth was a huge old bear, the largest that Katerina and Daniel had ever seen. He was standing up and he was salivating and growling. It was Ivan the Terrible. Hanging back a little was another mature bear; it was Oskar.

Nikitin's face was leaden. He appeared to begin to pray. He cowered in an undignified heap.

The scientist started speaking again,

"Ivan... no... leave be." Ivan the Terrible appeared to look him in the eye. "It won't help. Go home." He paused,

"Oskar, set a good example please. Lead Borodin and Ivan home."

Oskar and Borodin disappeared between the trees. Ivan the Terrible still stood there drooling.

"Hey, bear... hey, old pal," said the scientist moving between Ivan the Terrible and Nikitin. "You don't really want to eat us, do you? Lizabetta's been making cakes... and Doc has some honeycomb... you just go home."

The old bear looked confused but made a huffing noise and lumbered off after Oskar and Borodin.

Nikitin remained on the ground sobbing while Dr Joseph greeted the scientist.

"Well, hello, old friend... they said you had disappeared," he said giving the scientist a big hug.

"Whoa," said the scientist. "This is a surprise. You have found me out! I am living with my friends the bears. Katerina can tell you more, but can we please concentrate on getting rid of this intruder?" He pointed at Nikitin.

Katerina agreed she would tell Dr Joseph all about the situation if he would keep it secret. Then Daniel Joseph and Katerina manhandled a snivelling Nikitin down the track and the scientist headed back to Bearswood End. They bundled him into their vehicle and drove away.

"What are we going to do with him?" asked Katerina. "He might say something?"

"Say what?" said Dr Joseph with a big grin on his face showing the whites of his teeth. "That he was a big snivelling coward? If he says a thing, I will personally make sure his behaviour gets all over the Press and back to his President... I even have pictures..." He patted his pocket, although Katerina was sure he never took any pictures.

"Hey, Konstantin. If we re-unite you with your security, can you and your men take the first flight back to Russia?" Dr Joseph carried on. Nikitin nodded that he agreed.

"Konstantin, are we agreed nothing happened involving you and bears?" Nikitin nodded in agreement. "And will you tell your men that loggers accidentally set off a detonator? And that a bear was spooked and that if they say anything you will tell everyone they abandoned you?" He nodded in agreement.

Dr Joseph said, "I want to hear you say, 'yes, I agree to what Godfrey has said'."

Nikitin said dejectedly, "I agree to your terms, Godfrey. I hope never to be reminded of this again."

They found Nikitin's men and vehicle at the hunting camp. The explanation about the detonator was given to the 'heavies' and the guide. When the guide asked what the rest of them were doing there Daniel chipped in and said, "We followed you up to ask you not to hunt. We are not in favour of hunting. Whoever had a detonator was careless."

Dr Joseph's dark face nearly went red, and they left as soon as they saw Nikitin and his men were hurriedly going.

"This has been great fun," said Dr Joseph. "What a shame it has to be a secret."

The rest of the away leg was totally uneventful and soon the delegates were on their way back to Geneva. Konstantin Nikitin returned to Russia and Katerina and Daniel stayed behind.

Epilogue

It was mid-winter approaching Christmas and I received the following email which followed up some brief communication to let me know my daughter was safe and well.

'Dear Mum

The wonders of satellite communication means that off-grid or not I can wish you a very Happy Christmas. Daniel and I are safe and snug in Bearswood End.

We have taken on one of the old houses, making sure that it was not anyone's winter den. We have made it snug by putting in a huge amount of insulation. Daniel is a wizz at DIY and fitted some internal panels in our house and filled the void with insulating material. He repaired the chimney and the stove before winter, and we have a huge store of logs.

Your friend the scientist, as you call him (I use the professor's name), and Lizabetta are very well, and we share resources and dare I say it even socialise together. Doc was delighted by our arrival. His arthritic legs trouble him to some degree but psychologically his well-being is much improved. Wheels and Stores were suspicious of us at first, but now I think they feel confident enough to leave for a while in the spring so that Wheels can have further attention to his eyes. We have a plan and hopefully by the end of next summer they will have returned once more, with Wheels having completed all such treatment.

As for the bears I truly believe I am amongst friends. Oskar and Jeremy accompany me when I go out into the field. They appear to be my self-appointed guardians. Jeremy is still learning to drive adapted vehicles. I have not had the courage to ride in a vehicle solely controlled by a bear, but I have been in a truck many times with Oskar at the wheel and Stores at his side.

The bears have an unfortunate weakness for baked goods. Before they largely went into hibernation, we nearly had an issue with inhabitants of the settlement. Peter the Great seemed to suss out when the baker's van was doing a delivery and broke into it when it was parked unattended. Fortunately, he did not stick around to meet the locals when he had had his fill! I saw online that local news media recorded the event and an inhabitant of the settlement had caught a glance of an "enormous bear". It was a good thing no-one gave chase as I think Peter has slowed down in recent times as I believe he is probably quite old for a wild bear.

Ivan the Terrible does not go far these days. He can be encouraged to stay in the village more easily than in the past, particularly if there is food involved.

Lizabetta was very worried about her favourite bears, but I have a solution. In the spring we are building a bread oven where we will bake occasional tasty treats for the bears. I will be able to plan the contents of these baked treats. I am sure some naturalists will not *approve but these animals have minds of their own. If I bake something on site with carefully chosen ingredients, it will surely be better for the bears in all respects.*

Daniel is loving every minute of our off-grid life. Since his granny died, he has no immediate family in the outside world. We both have a few connections at the university and also with Dr Joseph, and we obtained a small grant for research on Brown bears, without needing to reveal our location. We understand our project to study Brown bears living in close proximity to each other is to be treated as ongoing. We are expected to send scientific data from time to time but nothing else.

Despite the challenges of an off-grid winter I regret nothing about coming here other than being unable to visit Dad and you. Bearswood End is a remarkable village inhabited by remarkable bears. I have every intention of making my life here and looking out for the bears. This is plainly not the end of their story; it is just the beginning.

With all my love

Katerina'

Sources, Reference, and Acknowledgements

Nowadays there is much material online, but I did refer to *'Bears'* by Daniel Wood published by Whitecap Books Ltd and *'Bears Rulers of the Wilderness'* by Robert Elman published by W H Smith Limited (copyright Todri Productions Ltd). I was inspired by the delightful photographs in Suzi Esterhas' children's book *'Brown Bear'* published by Frances Lincoln Children's books.

Online I referred to:

northamericannature.com

www.bearsmart.com,discoverwildlife.com,

www.euronatur.org and wwf.panda.org.

Regarding the Thunder Bay area of Canada, I referred to www.ontarioparks.com and to a very useful document called *'Checklist of Mammals of Thunder Bay District'* revised in 2018 and published by the Thunder Bay Field Naturalists. This latter document contains a huge amount of cross-referencing material. Of course, the obligatory tourist material can be obtained from TripAdvisor about Thunder Bay and Toronto, but various elements of the Thunder Bay chapter were drawn from my own experiences.

My husband and I did go to Ouimet canyon, the Fort William historical park and the Kakabeca Falls. We did drive along the lonely highway by the Pigeon River, and we did see a moose and an eagle along that road. A young Black bear did enter the garden of the guesthouse and he did peer over the veranda. He did indeed play with the hanging basket in the garden.

Have I ever been to Bearswood End? Certainly not the village in the book. As a child, I used to visit my grandmother in a road in Beaconsfield, Buckinghamshire called Bearswood End. There were woods behind her house, and they certainly seemed a special place to me although I knew there were no bears there. Is there anywhere like the village of Bearswood End, and where is it? The answer to both these questions is, "Who knows?"

Printed in Great Britain
by Amazon

86787721R00068